IF I DISAPPEAR

E.L. FAIRE

PROLOGUE

AUDREY
Three Years Ago

It's as dark as death itself. All I smell is dirt. And blood. Coating the sides of my nostrils, I'm inhaling the stuff.

Where am I?

I grit my teeth against the searing pain, tearing its way over the entire back of my leg, racing up my spine and burning a path to my throat, as I shift all my weight to the left.

I raise a shaky hand as high as it will go and run my fingers down the stone wall, inch by inch, checking for something. Anything. A window. A loose bit of cement. A forgotten tool.

It all comes back to me at once. The curve of his back in the moonlight. The hint of sweat along his flesh. Those eyes.

"Help!" I scream to no one, my fingers flying over the grooves and bumps faster now, scraping against the stonework, digging, scratching, trying anything… because the more I remember, the more I know.

There is no way out.

CHAPTER 1

BLAKE
Present Day

No wonder people go crazy in snowstorms. This level of brightness could have Gandhi mixing tequila shots with his Xanax.

I look over at the driver's seat where my boyfriend's been making his "irritated face" for the last half an hour. I don't even think he realizes he's doing it, bunching his lips to the side and darting his eyebrows down.

"We've just gotta beat the storm," he says when he sees me staring at him.

"We will." I lean over and rest my head on his shoulder. I can tell he's tense. I run my hand into his opened puffer jacket, squeezing his shoulder a little as I push myself against my seatbelt so I'm even closer to him.

"Blake, please. I need to concentrate."

He motions to the windshield wipers that are whipping back and forth as fast as they can, but aren't really keeping up with the snow that's falling.

We can barely see the road in front of us.

I go back to my seat. We both know this is my fault.

I grew up in Los Angeles, so I can count on one hand the amount of times I've seen snow. I'm not even sure I've actually witnessed it actively snowing before.

And this is a lot.

The snow falls so fast it's dizzying, like swirling, white madness.

I should have packed the night before, but I still wasn't sure I was going. I had no idea how bad storms could get in the mountains. Or how suddenly they could occur.

We inch our way around another bend; the cliff to our right is a sheer death drop. All I see are treetops and jagged rocks piercing through the clouds and snow. If the tires slip even a little, we're goners.

"Be careful," I say, bracing myself against the dashboard, almost breaking one of my nails.

"I *know*." Corbin's face bunches up again. "If we would've left when we were supposed to…"

"How many times do you want me to say I'm sorry, Corbin?"

I go back to the window, pressing my face against the cold glass, watching as my breath fogs up the little spot around my mouth. He doesn't usually snap at me like that.

But he's been snapping all day, saying things like, *"What do you mean you don't know what to pack? Just throw some clothes together and let's go."*

Our radio went out about ten miles back, and so did the Bluetooth, which Corbin told me was normal.

A friend of a friend of his owns the cabin, so he's been up here many times before. He knows what to expect with snow and no cellphone coverage and storms and cliff drops.

I had no idea.

All I know is we've been the only car on the road for a while, and the sun is setting. It was supposed to be a three- hour drive from Middleton. It's been more like six, with a stop to put chains on, and another one to fix the chains. And we're not even close yet.

I know he wishes he hadn't invited me on this trip. I was actually surprised when he did. Or maybe I invited myself. I hinted, but Corbin usually isn't the type who picks up on things like hints.

I wanted to see the cabin he always talks about before the owners put it on the market. It sounded so charming. Early 1900s vacation home remodeled in the 90s.

What did that even mean?

And I wanted to meet his friends.

All three of my brothers joked that I was probably Corbin's first girlfriend. *"I'm getting incel vibes, Blake,"* my oldest brother said like he's one to talk in the awkward department. *"Does he have friends outside of internet chat rooms?"*

Corbin seems to notice I'm upset, and he turns and smiles at me. "We're going to be fine. We're almost to town, and it's a straight shot from there. No more cliffs."

His eyes go to me, then the road, then to me again.

"I'm sorry I snapped," he adds. "I'm nervous, that's

all. Bear Landing's probably only ten minutes away now. We'll stop and get some gas and food. There's a grocery store. I'll check the tire chains again, too. And the cabin's only a few miles from town."

I worry that if we stop, we won't be able to start again because, from the looks of it, a lot of snow can fall during even a short stop. But I don't say this to Corbin. I can tell by the way the crease in between his eyebrows is deepening that he can only take so much right now.

I kiss his cheek so he'll feel better about snapping at me.

And he's right. It *is* my fault we're in this mess. Plus, he's doing all the stressful stuff, like putting chains on and driving. He's absolutely the best thing that has ever happened to me.

The whole move to Middleton was.

I am notorious for making completely spontaneous decisions that are usually pretty bad in hindsight. But I actually made a good one when I decided to move to the desert a little more than a year ago… for a guy that was not Corbin and did not work out.

My friends told me I was crazy to uproot myself from a stable career in Los Angeles (pharmaceutical sales, but I absolutely hated it) just to follow some guy I met online. And when I think about it, it *was* crazy.

I was making a great salary. I even drove a company car, for crying out loud, and all I had to do was peddle samples through LA traffic.

And I knew I wasn't in love with Chris when I moved in with him three months after we met. He wasn't in love with me either. We were just "roommates with benefits," and we both knew it.

But I wanted a change.

Still, I spent most of my time looking for a job, hanging out in coffee shops, sprucing up my resume and pretending to go on interviews. Basically, avoiding the guy while blowing through my savings.

That's when I met a gorgeously geeky tech guy with blonde tousled hair and a crooked smile who looked straight out of a rom com.

I couldn't break up with my roommate fast enough.

And now, seven months later, I think that geeky tech guy might be about to pop the question.

This weekend.

It has to be why he let me come along.

He's been carrying an engagement ring around in his backpack for the last month (I checked).

But, despite packing all my cute clothes and getting a manicure in case he *did* pop the question, I'm not sure how I feel about it.

It was why I took so long packing. *Is he really the one?*

"We made it," he says as a town comes into view. Or it might be a town.

I can't really tell with all the snow. Either way, it doesn't feel at all like "we made it."

As we get closer, I see there's not much to this place. Just a small, dark grocery store with no cars in the lot, only snow drifts. The diner next to it looks equally as abandoned, and across the street from that, there's a gas station where some guy in the window of the mini-mart is flipping the Open sign to Closed.

"Shit," Corbin says under his breath. "Everything's closing early because of the storm."

I tense up, expecting him to lecture me again on why we're so late getting up here, but he doesn't.

"If we hurry, I bet we can talk the guy at the gas station into letting us grab a few supplies," he says.

A bad feeling washes over me, creeping up my spine and across my chest. I do not want to go into that gas station.

I am not someone who ever gets *that feeling*. I never know when bad things are about to happen, but I'm getting that feeling right now as we roll under the awning covering the gas pumps.

The sky has significantly jumped in darkness in the last few minutes of our drive. Just ten minutes ago, I thought we'd reach the cabin before things got pitch black, but now I know we won't.

Corbin stops at a pump, zips up his puffer jacket, and cuts the engine. As if on cue, the wind pummels the side of the jeep, rattling the windows, shaking the entire thing, reminding me just how cold it's going to be when I open the door.

"You should go to the bathroom here if you need to. It might take a little while to make it to the cabin, even though it's close. We're going to be inching it."

"I thought we were stopping at a grocery store."

"That's the grocery store, Blake," he says, pointing across the street to the dark, empty parking lot. "It's not open." Even though he doesn't say it, his eyes blame me. "Just grab something here. Or take your chances. There's always food at the cabin."

I look at the rundown mini-mart beside me with so many advertisements for cigarettes and beer I can hardly see the windows. The Olsen Mart.

I need to use the bathroom, that's for sure. And I can't go on the side of the road, not that I ever could, but I definitely will not be doing that in the snow.

Still, I can't get myself to open the door. It's not just because I know it's going to be cold. There's also that niggling feeling that we shouldn't be here. That I shouldn't be here.

This is a bad idea, and we should go back.

But there is no turning back now.

CHAPTER 2

"What if they don't let us in?" I ask, as I pull my cotton gloves out of my pocket and slip them over my fingers. My hands don't feel any warmer, and I haven't even stepped outside yet. "The sign says *Closed.*"

"This isn't LA, Blake. People are nice in small towns. I'm sure they saw us drive up. Plus, this is your only option. Just go and make it quick. Grab some food, too."

And with that, he opens the driver's side door, and hops out, and I get a small taste of the freezer that awaits me.

My teeth chatter even after the door closes again.

While Corbin pumps the gas, I stare off at the store and the snow falling around it, trying to get myself to reach for the door handle.

Even though my boyfriend's head is down whenever the wind picks up, I can tell he's making the face again, wondering why I'm not doing exactly what he told me to do. And being quick about it.

He can be a little bit of a control freak at times, but this time, he's right. We're in the middle of a bad snowstorm, and I need to hurry before it really hits us.

I zip up my jacket and pull the hood over my head so it covers as much of my exposed skin as possible, tucking all the strands of my long blonde hair into the back of it before kicking open the door.

It's just as cold as I thought it'd be. The wind beats on my back like it can't wait to show me who's really in control of my body now, shoving me away from the car and over to the mini-mart.

The snow isn't so bad under the awning that's covering the gas pumps, but as soon as I step out from under it, I realize just how deep it is.

I am actually *trudging* through several inches. It's taller than my boots in some spots, especially around the parking spaces where it's already been plowed into weird drifts. It dampens the legs of my jeans and seeps into the top of my socks, making me realize my new knockoff duck boots might only be good for rain.

Every fourth step seems more like a slide that could send me toppling down. And who knew snow could feel like sand smacking your face when the wind picks up?

I do. I know now.

I finally manage to reach the front door of the Olsen Mart. I yank on the handle, preparing myself for what to say to the people who own this place.

The door doesn't budge. I try pushing and pulling. It's locked.

They saw us pull up to the gas pumps, I'm sure of it. So if they have no problem taking our money for gas, they should also let me use the facilities.

I knock on the window, peeking in the little spot between the Marlboro and Budweiser posters. I only see darkness on the inside.

"Hello?" I yell, knocking again. "I just saw you closing up. Do you mind if…"

"We're closed," a man's voice on the other end of the door yells to me.

I try to catch my boyfriend's eye to wave him over to help me, but he's waiting inside the jeep now where it's warm.

"I know. I'm sorry. Please. We just need to use the bathroom for a second and buy a few things."

"I said we're closed."

I lean against the door, trying to picture what I'll do if he really doesn't let me in to use the bathroom. Could I pee on the side of the building? My pee would freeze mid stream. I'm sure of it. And I don't like to picture the body parts that would freeze along with it.

I'm just about to hurry back over to the jeep when a face appears in the window. A bald man about 70.

He looks past me to our car at the gas pump, scrunches his face up, and groans. But I hear the door unlock. "Do I know you two?" he asks as he swings the door open.

I step inside before he can change his mind.

"No, but thank you so much for letting us in." I take my gloves off and stomp my boots on the long reddish gray mat at the front door. "I swear I will make this fast."

"Bathroom's that way," he says. He watches me slowly

walk over to it, slipping a little on the wet spots I'm creating on the linoleum.

Three minutes later, when I come out of the restroom, I expect to see Corbin, but he's not in the mini-mart.

I glance out the one window without advertisements. He's checking the chains on the jeep.

A 70-year-old woman has joined the 70-year-old man now. They're both standing at the cash register, watching me. They remind me a little too much of that American Gothic painting, minus the pitchfork that I'm one-hundred percent sure is somewhere behind the counter with them.

"Closing in two minutes," the woman yells.

The place is smaller than it looks on the outside. Dimly lit and it smells like bleach.

"If the coffee's cold, you can nuke it," the man says when he sees me pouring a cup. The woman whispers something to her husband.

They are watching me the entire time, while simultaneously glancing out at the gas pumps.

I put my coffee in the microwave and hit the number one. Then I head over to the snack aisle. I grab a bag of trail mix, a couple cans of Diet Coke, some Pringles, two plastic sleeves of tiny powdered donuts, and a small salad from the nearby refrigerated section, checking the date to make sure it's still good.

Surprisingly, it is.

I have no idea how long it will be before the grocery store opens up again, but I am taking no chances. What if we get stuck on the way up to the cabin and we have to do something like sleep in the car?

Why isn't Corbin in here, picking out snacks and using the restroom?

I briefly think about getting him something. But he is quite capable of coming in here and getting something himself.

And that's kind of a sore spot I will never admit to having. But it's more than annoying how much he expects me to do for him.

I place all of my things on the counter in front of the couple, then add a pack of gum, catching sight of myself in the reflection of the glass.

"Where you heading?" the man asks.

The woman doesn't nod or talk. She just works her jaw as she scans my stuff.

"My boyfriend's friend owns a rental cabin somewhere around here, or it's a friend of a friend, I don't know. They're putting it up for sale soon. So we're coming for the weekend…"

They exchange a quick look. The woman scans faster.

Just stop talking, Blake. These people don't really care about you or your boyfriend or the cabin you're on your way up to. You're babbling again.

"Better get going before the storm really hits," the man says.

"That'll be eighteen fifty-three," the woman adds.

I get my credit card out. She points to a sign that says "Cash Only."

I dig through my purse until I find a couple of tens. "You can keep the change," I say, like that's a big tip.

"Thank you again for letting me use your bathroom and get some food."

My stuff has been thrown into a thin plastic bag except for the coffee, and the man hands it out to me as I prepare myself to step into the freezer again.

They both follow me to the door.

The woman's gaze doesn't leave the window until she reaches the wall by the lottery station, where she finally looks up. I follow her eyes to the bulletin board full of "missing" and "found" dog posters, along with ones about tutoring and guitar lessons.

She seems to be looking at the faded missing-person poster in the mix.

I tug my phone out of my pocket and take a quick photo of the board without them seeing me. But I must not be moving fast enough for the man because he turns and opens the door, making cold air hit all of us.

"Thanks again," I say as I step outside, listening as the door closes behind me, and the lock clicks.

The wind is even worse than before because I'm walking against it now. It whips my coat, sending my bag of supplies smacking hard along my side.

Corbin doesn't notice me walking up, trying not to fall in what I now know are completely inappropriate rain boots. He's just waiting in the idling jeep with exhaust pouring out of the back of it.

He finally looks over when I'm about five feet from the passenger's side. He hops out and runs to open the door, but his "run" is more like a slow walk with hurrying arm movements.

I hand him my stuff while I get in, never more

thankful for a warm car in my life. My cheeks are already stinging and my nose is running.

"Missed your chance to go to the bathroom or get some snacks," I say when he gets back into the driver's seat. "I think that couple isn't about to let anyone else in today."

"I don't have to go, and I still have half a sandwich left from our last stop. I'll be fine. We should get moving."

He pulls out, our tires slipping a little on the snow-covered parking lot.

"They were kind of acting strange," I say. "Looking out at your car and stuff. Do you know the locals?"

He shakes his head. "Nope. I'm pretty sure the whole town is strange, though. You have to be strange to live this far from everything."

I look back at the Olsen Mart as we pull out of the lot and into the storm again, wondering if that's the last bit of civilization I will see for a while.

The couple looks out at us from their one uncluttered window.

CHAPTER 3

When Corbin said we were going to be inching it, I never thought he meant literally.

We sit in silence, or near silence as our tires grind and crunch over what I'm hoping is road. Corbin's muttering has picked up, too.

It's funny how you don't realize how much noise is around you until your usual stuff gets cut off. And you can't stream music or videos. Or even the radio anymore.

I bring out my phone and check the picture I took at the mini-mart, cropping it so I only see the missing-person poster.

Her long brown hair is pulled back in a neat ponytail. Her blue eyes are full of life as she smiles at the camera.

Missing
Have You Seen This Person?
Audrey Randall

Age: 23
Height: 5'7"
Weight: 130
Hair: Brown
Eyes: Blue
Last Seen: Cross country skiing between Jackson Mill and Landing Ski Resort
Reward: $3,000

Corbin looks over. "What's that?"

"An old poster of a missing woman." I turn my phone so he can see it better.

He glances at it, then goes back to the road. "Where did you get that?"

"The Olsen Mart. The couple there kept looking at the poster, so when they looked away, I took a photo…" I zoom in on the woman's face. "Do you remember hearing about her?" I hold out the zoomed-in version to him.

He doesn't look at it this time. "A little. There's not a lot of crime that happens in Bear Landing, so she was all anyone talked about three years ago. I think she was only up here because she was hiding from police. The old Missy Lagdon case. You know Missy Lagdon, right?"

I do. Everyone does. She was one of the first influencers back in the day when YouTube was just starting out. I was a kid then, mesmerized by all the crazy videos regular people would post online.

Most of them were cute and funny, like dance routines or cartoons. Some were cruel and degrading.

Missy's *Makeup for Freckles* video still stands out as one of the cruelest. And it had gone viral.

She and her friend basically tortured some poor neighborhood kid while pretending to do his makeup, duct-taping him to a chair, jabbing him in the eyes and ears with various tools, even some scissors, until the kid had a panic attack and shit himself.

All I really remember from the video is him squirming in the mess to get out of the duct tape.

It was like you could smell the video.

It had catapulted her to success. And then years later, as an adult, Missy Lagdon made the news again when her husband was murdered.

"She was *not* a nice person," I say.

Corbin points to my phone. "Well, that's the girl they think murdered Missy's husband."

He grips his hands tighter over the steering wheel, as the windshield wipers screech along the glass.

"What do you think happened to her?" I ask.

"Who? Missy or Audrey?"

"Audrey. Did they find her?"

"I don't think so." He wipes the sheen of sweat from his forehead with the back of his hand. "But she probably fell in a well. Woke up a hibernating bear. Hypothermia. Who knows? And who cares? Maybe she skipped town like some people say and is living the life in Mexico." He shakes his head. "I can't believe you took a picture of that."

His voice is curt now. I can tell he doesn't want to talk about this. I'm distracting him, and he needs to concentrate on the road.

Still, I hate how he belittles me sometimes.

"I was just bored, I guess." I put my phone away and

stare out the window, noticing we've reached a stretch of houses now, if they can be considered houses. They're more like the old forgotten carcasses of what used to be houses. Boarded-up shacks with snow-covered junk cars in their front yards.

I have plenty of time to notice them with how slowly we're moving.

We approach Landing Ski Resort, which is really only rusty poles and forgotten chair lifts now.

One of the chairs blows in the wind, creaking and snapping against its cable. It's covered in about six inches of snow.

"The ski resort closed more than ten years ago," he says. "A lot of people left after that, I guess."

Corbin seems to notice the face I'm making as I look around. "Stop worrying. We're fine. You'll see. The cabin is much nicer than this. There's a tree swing and a hill perfect for sledding. I can't wait to show you how to cross-country ski. You're gonna pick it up, no problem. You love ice skating, right? It's similar to that. You just kind of shift your weight from side to side and glide."

I point out the window. "We're gonna be able to do all of that in *this* snowstorm?"

"It might let up."

Plus, I never told Corbin this, but ice skating was never my thing. My brothers tried to make it my thing for two full years before giving up. They were die-hard hockey players, but I was a sulky teen who only wanted an iPhone.

"We can also just chill in the cabin. The place is always stocked with food," he goes on. "I'm talking a freezer full of veggies and frozen pizzas. Cookies and crackers in the pantry. Wine. They really only rent it out to friends now, so it's pretty homey."

I smile, thinking about the twenty bucks I wasted on donuts and soda. No wonder he didn't buy anything.

"We'll spark up the jacuzzi. Have some wine and maybe watch some of the old DVDs they always have in one of the baskets by the TV that probably hasn't been touched in ages."

"DVDs…" I say, already feeling nostalgic. He warned me last week that we'd be living in 1996 all weekend without internet or cellphone coverage. But I never once thought of it as a bad thing.

After what feels like hours of slogging along, Corbin finally points to the street to our left. "It's just up this hill," he says.

The "hill" is a steep incline filled with snow, with no other houses around.

And instead of turning onto the street like normal, he backs the car up to the very bottom of it, like he's psyching himself up to tackle the drive.

"I was hoping the snowplow would've come by," he says. "But if we get stuck, we're close enough to walk."

"I am not walking up this hill in this snow."

"Then you'd better keep your fingers crossed that we don't get stuck." The engine grinds as the back wheels slide this way and that behind us, but eventually we're moving forward up the hill toward a large, two-story cabin at the top.

I can see its wood paneling peeking out of the snow and trees. It's redwood colored with a deck. Much better than most of the other cabins I've seen so far, thank God, but that's not saying much. That bar was set very low.

And at least those other cabins were close to other people. This one is a couple miles off the beaten path.

I search around the trees for signs of life, but it seems like there's nothing but shadowy limbs for miles in all directions.

His friends aren't even here yet, from what I can tell.

That's when I hear the engine whine and cough underneath us, shaking the jeep, only we're no longer moving. The wheels are spinning, but we're not going anywhere. Corbin moves the steering wheel around, trying to free us from our stuck spot.

"Sorry," he says, as he sets the brake. "I think we're gonna have to walk."

"We're only halfway up."

"I know that, babe. There's nothing I can do. Good thing neither one of us brought a ridiculous 100-pound rolling suitcase that's larger than most pieces of furniture."

"It's carry-on size," I shoot back.

"Do you want to carry it? Because it's not rolling in this snow. And I've got too many things I've already got to carry."

I stare down at my knock-off duck boots. I'm not prepared for any of this, including my boyfriend's attitude.

"We're going to have to leave most everything here. We can come back for some stuff tomorrow when it's light, and the storm has let up," he says. "If the storm has let up."

I zip my coat up again and lift the hoodie over my head.

"Is there another option?" I ask.

"Sleep here. Wait and hope for a snowplow. We can make our own warmth..." he says with a gleam in his eye.

He's not serious.

"Look, it's not going to take us very long to walk to the cabin. And I'll try calling the snowplow company on the landline as soon as we get in the house. I promise," he says, lifting my chin gently in his hand. He presses his lips over mine.

And I pull him in closer, not wanting to let go.

"We're going to be fine," he adds, again.

But the more he says we're going to be fine, the farther I feel from it.

My backpack with my laptop is in the front seat by my feet. I unzip the pouch and stuff my bag of snacks into it, along with my cellphone cord and headphones.

He looks at me, like he's mentally asking if I'm ready to go, but then turns the car off before I can mentally reply no.

He trudges to the back of the jeep. I take a deep breath and hop out too, surprised by how far my boots sink into the snow and how quickly my toes feel numb when that happens.

By the time I get around to the back, Corbin's got my suitcase unzipped, and he's rifling through my things.

I step in front. "Hey," I say. "That's mine."

"I know. I stuffed some of my things in there last second. You have a lot of extra room."

"You should have asked," I say.

"I did, just before we left."

I am too tired and cold to argue with him. My feet are already freezing, and my nose is running.

And honestly, I don't know why I'm being so defensive, anyway. We're practically married now. What's mine is his, and vice versa. Plus, I did just go snooping through his backpack on a successful ring-finding mission, so I really don't have a leg to stand on here.

Still, I have a lot of trust issues, and there's something I don't quite trust about my boyfriend. I've been telling myself it's all in my head for a while now.

But this weekend is when I'll be deciding if it is.

Corbin tucks a couple of his sweatshirts into his duffle bag. "You can put some things in here, if you want. I'll carry it."

"Thanks."

He moves out of the way, and I quickly grab a couple pairs of underwear, a pair of jeans, and some soft socks, my pajamas, some sweats and my toiletry bag, then zip the suitcase back up again.

Corbin grabs a shovel and his duffle bag, and I grab his backpack, but it feels like it's full of bricks. I set it back down again.

"I got it," he says, then takes my backpack too.

"You sure? I can carry something."

"You just worry about walking through this snow," he says, kissing the very top of my forehead, and my toes suddenly don't feel as cold anymore. He is so thoughtful.

He starts up the hill like a pack mule, and I follow behind, taking long inhales while trying to control my breathing so I don't sound winded, even though I already am.

Lifting my legs in and out of the snow is a lot of work on a steep incline.

Plus, I've only been up in the mountains a couple of times before, but it was enough to know the air is thinner up here. It doesn't take much to become light-headed and out of breath.

All I hear is the sound of our breathing, growing heavier as we crunch step by step.

I lift my eyes up to the sky, and almost fall over from the swirling, dizzying mass of white coming down at me, blinding me.

Corbin looks back and sees me trying to catch a flake on my tongue. "I knew you'd like it here," he says.

"Yeah, this could be fun," I say, but I'm not sure I mean it.

My thighs ache and I haven't been able to feel most of my body for the last ten minutes by the time we finally reach the driveway.

"The key pad's around back," Corbin announces as he walks by the front door and heads around to the side.

Nothing is lit, not even a porch light.

And as I round the corner to the back, I realize there aren't neighbors back here either, just more dark patches of woods.

Corbin sets all the bags down on the porch and rests the shovel against the siding. He flicks on his cellphone light and hunches over the keypad there.

The smell of a nearby fire wafts up with the wind. "Do you smell that?" I ask. "So, there *are* neighbors?"

He sniffs. "There's only one I know about, and he's a couple miles away. Let's just say we'll be avoiding that guy."

The way he says that last part makes me think Freddie Krueger is our only neighbor, which would be fitting for this place.

Corbin doesn't look up from the keypad as he punches in numbers and tries the door, but nothing happens. "That's not it either," he mutters. We both know if he doesn't remember how to get in, there's no cell-phone coverage to text his friend, and we'll have to trudge back down to the car to sleep.

I dance from foot to foot, trying my best not to seem impatient. He hates it when I hurry him. I look out at the night instead.

The backyard itself is the size of a farm, or what this city girl pictures "farm-size" being. It's easily ten times bigger than my parents' house in LA.

You got your money's worth up here.

He glances over at me. "Don't worry. The old mill separates us from that neighbor…" he says, like he thinks I was worrying. I wasn't, until he said that last part.

"The old mill? And there's part of the ski resort over here, too. So you're saying, this is the *exact* area the woman from the missing poster was last seen at, Corbin?"

He doesn't answer me. He has the door open now.

"Let the weekend begin," he says, stepping inside.

CHAPTER 4

Corbin stomps into the dark hallway, but glances back at the keypad. "It's 9354," he says. "Remember that, in case you need it."

9354, I repeat to myself as I follow him inside.

The first thing I notice, aside from the fact it's not much warmer inside, is the smell.

It has the musty, dank smell of an abandoned house.

He flicks on a light. "Welcome to paradise," he says. I can see his breath forming a little cloud in front of his face as he talks.

"Paradise is usually at least seventy degrees."

"I'll go adjust the thermostat," he says and walks off, his boots making a thudding noise over the floorboards as he passes the bathroom by the backdoor. "It's always a little cold at first. Unless someone's renting the place, the owners just leave the heat at 'warm enough so the pipes don't freeze.'"

There's a coat rack in the hall by what looks like a

back bedroom, along with a sign next to it requesting I remove my shoes. But I ignore both the sign and the rack and stomp a trail of snow down the hall toward the kitchen, in my coat and boots.

It seems strange to be in this cabin when Corbin doesn't own it. And he's only kind of friends with the person who does.

It's a nice place, though. Cozy and normal. Much more normal than I thought it was going to be.

The kitchen is larger than the one we have in our apartment in Middleton.

I open the fridge. It's empty. I open the freezer. Empty too.

So much for the pizza I was promised.

I walk over to the pantry. *Please let this pantry be filled to capacity with wine and crackers.*

There are only trash bags, bleach, and a broom.

I try not to feel resentful that I'm going to have to share my donuts and soda now.

Corbin's talking to me from the living room. "There. I set it at paradise level. That ought to do it. But I'll make a fire, too," he says, and I follow his voice to the next room.

As I pass the sink, I notice it has dishes in it, which is strange. A couple of plates and a glass with lipstick on the side of it, with water at the bottom.

Why didn't the rental cabin get cleaned after the last guests?

But then, maybe one of his friends made it up here, then left to get supplies. That has to be it.

Except I don't remember seeing any signs of another person. No footsteps in the snow. No tire tracks either.

"There are dirty dishes in the sink," I say.

"What? That's gross. They were supposed to clean."

"Well, *they* didn't."

"Maybe the house cleaners couldn't come in the snowstorm. The snow's been falling like crazy for a while. I'll clean the dishes."

He hurries across the room and over to the sink.

"The sheets might be dirty too, then," I call after him. "If the housecleaner didn't come, who knows?"

He doesn't answer me, so I join him in the kitchen, where he's standing over the sink, looking at the lip gloss on the side of one of the glasses.

"If you make the bed, I'll clean the dishes," I say.

He looks up at me, but it seems to take him a second to process what I've said. He sets the glass back down. "You cannot be serious. You want me to remake the bed?"

"Only if it looks like it needs it." I give him my best puppy dog face. I know he can't resist that.

He shakes his head, but a hint of a smile dances on his lips. "Deal, I guess, even though I'm pretty sure you got the better end of the stick on that one, germaphobe," he says. "There are only a few dishes."

"Deal's a deal," I say, looking around, wondering why anyone would rent this place, much less buy it.

It's absolutely charming, don't get me wrong — spacious, yet small enough not to lose its coziness, and everything is accented in wood, including the ceiling beams and the paneling on some of the walls.

But we're in the middle of nowhere. And there's not even a ski resort anymore.

I've probably just seen too many horror movies back when I was 11 and trying to gross out my brothers. But a lot can happen in a secluded cabin.

I move past the coffee table that's actually a sliced-down-the-middle tree trunk shellacked to a shiny, glass-like finish and turn on one of the lamps on the end table, realizing it was whittled out of wood to look like a bear, because when you own a rental cabin in Bear Landing, you have to feature bears in the decor.

Everything is 90s, all right, from the bears that watch your every move, to the fake plants, to the overstuffed couches.

And the lamp doesn't even do much to brighten the room. It just creates a strange yellow cast over the furniture.

"Looks like they still have the DVDs," Corbin says, pointing to a basket under the flatscreen.

"Nice," I say and head over to it.

The Lion King, Aladdin, Honey, I Shrunk the Kids. I pull a couple out. Cracker crumbs fly out with them. A lot of crumbs. *Did all of that come from the basket?* They're scattered along the floorboards and the off-white Oriental rug. I'll have to sweep now, too.

Warm air pours out of a vent by my feet, but I know it's going to be a while before it heats this place up.

Corbin is looking through one of the metal bins by the fireplace. He turns and notices me staring at cracker crumbs and walks over. "Quit worrying, okay?"

"I don't see any food or wine," I say. "I checked the fridge and the pantry."

"No. I'm sure there's food, but even if there's not,

that's okay. We're not going to starve." He points to the floor. "There are plenty of crumbs. If we sweep them all up, we'll have enough for days. And look, there's a little lint there, too."

He waits for me to smile at his joke, then he wraps his hands around the back of my head and pulls me into his chest. I love it when he does that. Such a sexy move. I almost don't mind that this time I'm pretty much inhaling his still-wet-from-snow puffer jacket.

"Don't forget my friends are coming up too, and they'll bring plenty of food. I'm really surprised they're not already here."

Neither one of us is saying the obvious. There's probably a text waiting for him when we get back into cell-phone range, saying they're not coming because of the storm.

Corbin is still talking. "They always bring way too much. And, I brought champagne." He kisses my forehead.

I look up into his hazel eyes. "You brought champagne?"

"Yeah, of course I did. Three bottles. I'm about to introduce my friends to the most amazing woman I've ever met. We need champagne to celebrate. The bottles are in the car, along with the beer I also brought. I'll go back out and get a few. I'll grab the rest of my sandwich too."

"You're not walking all the way back out to the car for champagne and a sandwich," I say. "That's crazy."

"I want to." He motions to the fireplace. "I have to go out, anyway. There's no firewood, as far as I can tell, which is weird because there's always firewood. But I'm sure there's some in the shed. Pick out the room you want us to sleep in while I'm gone. There's one downstairs and two upstairs. And see if you can find the phone number for the snowplow. It should be… somewhere. There might be a phone book, too."

We both laugh when he says "phone book." It *is* like we're living in 1996 right now. Landlines. DVDs. No internet.

Corbin scoops up his backpack and car keys from the coffee table and stomps his way through the kitchen again before I can protest too much about him leaving.

But then, I'm not protesting at all. I want champagne and a fire, and maybe even a reason to celebrate.

I stretch my hand out and study the empty spot on my ring finger, picturing the traditional solitaire I saw in his backpack last month. I glance up. Just behind my hand, I see a pair of skis propped against the wall on the staircase landing, and I think about the poster again.

Last Seen: Cross country skiing between Jackson Mill and Landing Ski Resort

I hear the back door open and close, and as soon as it does, I realize just how alone I am, in a house in the middle of nowhere, when everything seems off.

AUDREY
Three Years Ago

MY DESK LAMP IS JUST ABOUT THE ONLY LIGHT ON NOW that the office has powered down for the night. The last sounds come from the custodian, crinkling out a new bag for the trashcan in the hall by the elevator. He'll be gone soon.

Trash is the last thing he does before saying goodbye. I pretend to be looking at my laptop when he walks over five minutes later.

"They got you working late again?" he asks.

"Yeah, but I want to."

"Someone like you should be out barhopping on a Friday. You know that, right?"

I smile down at my keyboard. I know he means

"someone young." And I agree. Someone like me should be anywhere but here. "There's a big meeting on Monday…"

He lifts a hand, stopping me from going on too much. "No need to explain. You're not the first newbie I've ever met." He winks at me.

We both know I need this job. Why else would I work for shit pay and even shittier hours? It's barely enough to make the rent on my studio apartment. Thank God my landlady is kind of cool, saying things like, "Pay me the full amount next month when your job picks up."

Working for Missy Lagdon is a huge stepping stone, or so I've heard. And, honestly, I should be happy this place didn't do a thorough background check before I was hired.

"It'll get better," he says. "Stick with it."

"Have a nice weekend," I say, and he smiles out the same.

I wait until I know he's gone before I stand and stretch, lifting my hands over my head like I'm trying to touch one of the pock-marked ceiling tiles. There's a clock just above the coffee station. It's 10:15. He left early, so I have a little extra time.

The place looks different at night. I prefer it dark and deserted, where I can blend in with the shadows and not have to worry about things like making small talk about influencers I don't really follow. Or the latest Netflix show.

I can do cartwheels down this aisle if I want to.

I glance up at the camera stationed by the clock. It's still in the same position I moved it to last week. It's safe to go wherever I want.

Lagdon Marketing has an open floor plan with about seven desks in the strategy section alone.

I'm still in my probationary period, so I've got the smallest one in the back, but I don't mind. I make my way around all of them, stopping first at Joy's.

I reach my hand into the back of my bun, feeling for a bobby pin. I pull it out and bend it straight.

Two seconds later, and I'm opening Joy's locked desk drawer.

I pull out her planner, a couple of flash drives, and a portable toothbrush and place them all on the desk in front of me, then tug off the false bottom part of her drawer.

People always keep the good stuff in places like this. Joy's "good stuff" consists of money, receipts, truffles, a box of coffee pods… The woman does not trust the rest of us.

I lift out the box of Kani Gold coffee pods, which sell for more than $100 for a box of twelve. I know. I googled them.

She's not sharing these with the break room.

I've heard from others that Joy used to have an executive suite next to Missy's office, but she and Missy have been fighting lately. So she's here with the rest of us peons, and I can tell she resents it.

She's Missy Lagdon's longtime friend. There should be perks.

I can't help but think she's here for other reasons.

Lately, she's been asking a lot of questions. About my college. My sorority. My internships.

It's like she's taken it upon herself to bring up every

bullet point on my resume. And she should not have access to my resume.

She just doesn't know me very well yet. Mess with me, and I'll mess with you.

I grab her receipts and stuff them into my pocket, in case I need to use them against her someday. I always take those whenever I see them in people's desks. Everyone uses the company credit card for questionable stuff.

But Joy has the most questionable and expensive tastes around. And if she doesn't stop prying into my business, Missy's going to find out about it.

I pop one of the imported dark chocolate truffles into my mouth. It melts on my tongue. Silky, smooth, decadent. Just like the commercials I found about them on YouTube, translated from German.

I reach in my cardigan pocket and take out the golden-colored coffee pod I brought home with me yesterday and push it into its spot in the Kani Gold box, then replace the false bottom and everything else.

Exactly like it was before.

I inspect the desk one last time to make sure it looks right. Check that the bobby pin is in my cardigan next to the receipts, then move onto the other desks in my section.

I stop at Ryan's desk next and open his top drawer. A Rubik's Cube and two fidget spinners sit next to a couple of condoms. I close the drawer and move on. Nothing has changed since the last time. Nothing locked up and exciting.

Going through desks is the fastest way to get to know

people. I already feel so close to my coworkers. Like I know that Ryan and Joy used to have a thing, because there's a grainy polaroid of Ryan in the false bottom part of Joy's desk.

And I wouldn't know this about them if I didn't look through their stuff.

I also know that Ryan's good friend, CJ, likes to go through desks, too. Only he steals stuff. Brenda's missing hair clip? It's in CJ's desk. So are all the highlighter pens people keep asking about.

It was why I thought I could trust him. But I should have known better.

The first time I met him, he bragged about his tech skills, and how he used to be able to hack into computers back when he was in high school. *He should be in the IT department, really.* But then, I found out he had no idea we even had cameras in the office.

And they're all over the place here. Eleven, to be exact. One in the elevator. Four in the parking garage. The list goes on and on.

Thankfully, no one seems to check them. I've managed to move the angle on every single one several times without anyone noticing the difference.

I even got CJ to move one in the garage, before I realized he wasn't trustworthy.

I make my way by the coffee station at the front of the room, then down the hall by the bigwigs' offices.

I'm not worried about cameras tonight. I walk right down the middle until I reach the largest office in the back.

It's not locked. I knew it wouldn't be.

Missy Lagdon's office.

It's only fitting that the owner of the marketing firm should have the best office here. But my God, this makes the rest of us look like a trailer park.

There's a full-on sitting area with couches and a flat screen, a private bathroom off the side that I try to use every time I come in. Even one of those swanky bars you see on TV.

I don't turn on the light.

I could make my way around this place with my eyes closed by now if I wanted to. I walk over to the desk and slide into the soft leather of her chair. My bare legs stick to the cushion because, even though the heat got turned down a half an hour ago, it's still pretty warm in here.

The lights of downtown Middleton blink back at me from Missy's picturesque window.

I lean back, slip off my heels and prop my feet up on her desk, in between the two framed photos. One is of her accepting an award for "most likes" for her YouTube channel about ten years ago.

And the other is a silver-framed photo of her and her husband at their wedding where her blonde hair cascades over her shoulder while her husband dips her back.

I've never seen a man like him before in real life. Only in the movies. Dark hair, broad shoulders, soulful eyes.

But he's only looking at Missy. *Everyone loves Missy.*

Hard to believe I didn't even know who the woman was until I was about to interview for the job.

I glance over at the wardrobe in the back of the office, then hop up from the desk.

It's where Missy keeps her extra outfits. Louis Vuitton.

Gucci. There's a peach Chanel jacket I love to pull out and try on because I can almost hear my grandmother's voice behind me whenever I do it. *"You can't buy this shit at Walmart. This is quality."*

The tile feels good on my bare feet as I make my way over to the closet and swing the doors wide open to see what's new, because there's always something new when it comes to rich people. They never run out of stuff they want to buy themselves.

And luxury has a distinctive smell. I run a finger over the different fabrics, taking a long inhale when the clothes rustle together, making the hint of perfume grow stronger.

There's a nice arrangement in here. Purses. Shoes. Even carry-on bags she can pick up and stuff at a moment's notice.

I slide the hangers over so I can reach the back of the wardrobe, where she keeps the odd collection of about four pieces of lingerie.

The pieces don't look worn at all. They're all brand new with tags. Never seen by soulful eyes.

I pull out a short beige nightie and hold it up to my dress, smoothing it over my body.

Who buys negligees anymore?

There's a mirror on the inside door of the closet, and I pull the rest of the bobby pins out of my bun and slip them in my cardigan pocket, then toss my hair around so it falls down my shoulders on either side of the nightie.

I love how the sheer fabric brushes against my chin, how it seems to skim every curve in all the right places. I bet it feels amazing.

I drop the negligee and wiggle out of the cardigan and black dress I picked up for about twenty bucks on clearance at Old Navy, and kick them both over to the base of the wardrobe. I unstrap my bra and let it fall to my feet, then step out of my underwear next, until I'm standing in Missy's office completely naked. Right in front of the window.

It's not light enough in here for anyone to see me from outside, not as far back as I am while I stand by the wardrobe.

Yet, I let myself imagine that someone does.

"Audrey," a voice says from the top of the wardrobe. I look up, where a little camera sits that you'd never notice if you weren't looking for it. *"Remember, do it just like we talked about."*

CHAPTER 6

BLAKE
Present Day

The house is too quiet after Corbin leaves.

Aside from the wind that howls and whistles through the trees, there's really only the soft ticking of a clock somewhere and the sound of heat grumbling out of a nearby vent.

My back stiffens at every noise, picturing the worst. I've never lived alone for a reason. I have a very active imagination.

Friday the 13th. Child's Play. Nightmare on Elm Street. Blair Witch.

They're all coming back to haunt me now.

A thick curtain covers the sliding glass door leading out to the deck, and I pull it back and look out at the night. Snowy white trees obstruct my view of the car.

But I'm not sure I could see it from here, anyway.

I let the curtain fall back and look around the living room, deciding to pop in a DVD to lighten the mood with some background noise while I search this place over, top to bottom, for things like an all-important phone book.

I pull out *Honey, I Shrunk the Kids* from the basket and head over to the DVD player, pushing the power button, but nothing happens. I press it again, then check the back of the TV.

Great, it's missing its power cord. It's probably here somewhere. I sit down on the crumb-covered floorboards and search the wicker basket full of movies, digging around the DVDs, but I don't feel a cord.

So much for nostalgia.

I get up and head to the desk in the corner where I expect to see the phone book and a phone. But there's nothing there except decorative stuff, like candles and more bear statues.

I turn toward the kitchen. Nothing on the island or the wall, either.

Wind whips against the sliding doors again, rattling them this time. The light flickers a little, and my heart drops into my chest.

Please don't let the electricity go out.

I decide to add "flashlight" to my list of things to look for while I wait for Corbin.

I open the first drawer of the desk. Even though it's full of blank stationery and pencils, I lift everything up and look through it all.

No cord. No flashlight. No snowplow number. Or phone.

I go to the next drawer down. Home decor magazines from 2010, a deck of UNO cards, and a book. *Gulliver's Travels*, of all things.

I flip through each one, then put them all away and close the drawer.

There's only one thing in the third drawer. An old brown clothbound guest book.

I pull it out and check the sliding glass door one more time for Corbin.

I don't see him, but I do notice a large snow-covered lump to the right on the deck that I'm pretty sure has to be the jacuzzi.

I have no idea how to turn that thing on, or how long it will take to warm up once we do turn it on. But I do know we will be getting into it sometime this weekend, if the electricity doesn't shut off by then.

I plop down on the couch with the guest book.

There might be a note from the owners or something telling me where to find the phone and the DVD cord. Or at least that's what I'll tell Corbin if he comes in and sees me sitting around, looking at a guest book, instead of doing the exact thing he told me to be doing.

The room is starting to heat up, finally. I practically melt into the soft leather of the oversized couch.

It feels good to sit down, even though the only thing I've done for the last six hours is sit in a car and watch my soon-to-be-fiancé drive in a snowstorm.

And now he's walking all the way back down the hill to get champagne because I pouted about there not being wine.

He really *is* a keeper. Me? I'm the one of us who

complains about cracker crumbs and doesn't want to share her donuts, or even look for a phone book.

There's a basket by the couch with a green and brown crochet blanket folded in it. I take my puffer jacket off, then wrap myself in the afghan like a burrito.

The whole thing is itchy and smells like a thrift store, but it's the only blanket around, as far as I can see. I tug off my boots and let them fall to the floor by my feet, then curl up into the smell of dust and mothballs.

The guest book is thick with cream-colored pages and a brownish red cloth cover that says "Welcome to Bear Landing" on the front in a large swirly font.

I turn to the first page, where a generic introduction printed by the manufacturer greets you:

Dear Guests,

We sincerely hope you're enjoying your stay in beautiful Bear Landing, California. Please feel free to share your thoughts and memories of all the wonderful adventures you had during your visit in the pages of this book.

I flip to the first entry. It's from 1999, and I'm actually surprised it was that recent.

There are pre-filled suggested prompts printed on every page to make things easier for guests: Name, date of stay, weather, adventures, restaurants worth trying, etc.

I read the first entry.

Jim, Theresa, Tucker, and Handley

They didn't give a last name, but they stayed June 14-20 and enjoyed horseback riding and the visitors center because there's a little museum there with animal skulls that Tucker loved. They looked for the elusive old mill, but couldn't find it. *Maybe next time. Thanks for the fabulous stay! Who knew Bear Landing was also fun in the spring?*

I flick through the pages, skipping to the middle where I stop momentarily because several guests heard creaking noises coming from the attic and declared the place haunted. Others noted how dirty the house was.

Cracker crumbs are everywhere.

Some people saw rats in the kitchen. And roaches.

I lift my feet up from off the floor.

How are there still cracker crumbs now?

No wonder they're selling the place. Once you get a reputation for rats and roaches, it's really hard to come back from it.

I jump ahead to the newer pages, breathing a small sigh of relief that the ghost, roach, and rat entries seemed to end about 2014, but I still don't put my feet back down, just in case.

As the pages skim through my fingers, I notice something else, too.

There are underlined letters in some of the entries. Not all, just some. And some are underlined twice.

A code.

I check the book over. The underlines are mostly in the middle section. I don't see any past 2015.

I stand and walk to the desk and open the first drawer again, pulling out one of the pieces of dusty, gray stationery and a pencil.

Then, I sit back down on the couch in front of the guest book to look for the first underlined letter.

I write down all the ones with the single line under them first, beginning with an I.

I'm careful not to miss anything, searching one of the rat entries over for any more underlined letters. There are two more on that page. I write them down, in order.

IFI

I go to the next page, then the next, just as I hear the ceiling creak above me.

I gasp and look over toward the staircase, but I can't even see the landing from my spot on the couch.

Corbin is outside. That can't be him moving on the second floor.

I also know it could be my imagination. Houses shift all the time, or so I've heard. Probably they do a lot more in snow storms. Or when someone with lip gloss is squatting in your rental.

Or when there are rats.

I freeze and listen. After a minute of staring at the ceiling, I begin to feel silly. No one is there. I don't hear anything else.

I go back to the guest book. There are a lot of underlines in the next entry. Seven, but a couple are underlined twice. I decide to concentrate on the ones with only one line first.

It doesn't take long before a message forms on my paper, my breath catching when I see what I've scribbled so far.

IFIDISAPPE

If I disappear?

I quickly flip to the next page to confirm, just as a loud crash upstairs makes me jump, because it's followed by shuffling.

No mistaking it that time. Someone is here.

And Corbin is not.

CHAPTER 7

I bolt up from my spot on the couch. The crochet blanket falls from my shoulders, catching on my necklace, making me scream.

I yank it the rest of the way off and toss it over the guest book. I'm jumpy tonight, that's for sure. But that was more than my imagination.

I quickly walk away from the stairs and the noise, heading through the kitchen, and over to the backdoor, my socks hitting wet spots from melted snow along the way.

Swinging the backdoor open, I look out at the darkness and the snow. Anything could be lurking in the shadows out there.

I can't go out. But I also don't feel safe inside.

"Corbin," I call out.

He doesn't answer.

Even though the snow is falling quickly, I can still see

tracks around the yard. There are ones leading toward the driveway, but there are other tracks, too, that go out to the forest and the back of the yard. Even ones that lead around the opposite side of the house.

I squint to see them better.

Are they Corbin's or someone else's?

I step closer to them, leaving the door ajar as my warm, socked feet crunch and stick to the bits of snow on the back porch, my toes instantly going numb.

I lean forward. The tracks go everywhere.

"Corbin!" I yell again. This time, a little louder.

I hear something behind me, and I turn quickly, but I'm too late. It was the door, shutting.

Like someone closed it.

I feel my heart racing into "horror movie" mode, and I remind myself to calm down. There are logical explanations for everything, and I don't need to freak out, even though I'm in socked feet in a snowstorm, at night.

The door closed because of a draft from the furnace fan. Not a killer.

I reach for the knob, but the door must lock automatically when it closes, because it doesn't budge.

You know the code, Blake. 93… something.

It takes me a second to remember it, but it finally comes.

9354. 9354.

I slowly punch it in. But the door doesn't unlock.

I punch it in a little faster the second and third time.

I take a deep breath. *This code didn't work for Corbin the first few times either, Blake. The keypad's probably glitchy.*

I put it in one more time. Still nothing. I try a different combination of the same numbers, reversing the last two. My hands are starting to shake. I curl and stretch my fingers out, then cup both hands around my mouth and blow on them to warm up.

My hands don't feel any warmer when I'm done. I know I have to be quick. I have no idea how long it takes for a human body to freeze in a snowstorm, but it can't be long. I decide it's best to try the code one more time before breaking a window, but I *will* be breaking a window if it comes down to it.

I don't care that his friend is selling the house. Whoever it is really needs to get this keypad fixed.

I look around for the shovel Corbin brought from the car so I can break the glass easier, but it's not under the keypad anymore.

That's funny.

"Blake, what in the hell are you doing? Babe?"

I turn. My boyfriend is standing behind me on the first step of the porch. Thank God. I run over to him and wrap my shivering body around his. His coat is cold and plastic feeling. He pulls away, unzipping the coat and pulling it off. He wraps it around my shoulders.

"How long have you been out here?"

"Three or four minutes, tops," I say.

"That's three or four minutes too long," he replies, like I don't already know that. "Why are you out here, anyway?"

"I heard a noise upstairs. It sounded like someone was in the house, so I stepped out onto the porch to see if I could find you. The door closed and locked…"

He's already at the keypad, punching in a set of numbers. He turns the lock, and the door opens for him.

"I don't know what I did wrong."

"Nothing ever works when you're panicking," he replies. "9359."

"You said 9354 earlier."

"Maybe you just misheard me." He shakes his head and goes inside. I follow closely behind.

"Good thing I saw you," he adds. "You could've died."

"I was going to break a window." My voice is weak. My whole argument is, and I feel silly again, especially with the way he's looking at me after hearing I was about to break his friend's window.

Corbin always tells me I freak out over nothing, and he might be right.

"Houses make noises, Blake."

"This one was different. Something crashed upstairs. I heard it."

I can tell by how slowly he's walking that he's listening for the "alleged noise" that he thinks was my imagination.

"Why didn't you at least put on some boots before you went outside?" He motions to the extra pair sitting under some ski masks at the coat rack as we pass it.

"I wasn't expecting to actually go outside. I was just going to open the door and yell for you."

He sets his backpack by the kitchen island and turns to me. "You look frozen," he says as he kisses my cheek. His eyes widen just a little. "You *are* frozen. Your cheeks feel like ice. Why don't you go sit on a heating vent while

I check for what made the noise? You should take those wet socks off."

I shake my head no. "I won't be able to relax until we've looked the house over together, especially not with the dishes in the sink and everything. And something definitely crashed. Something *broke*."

I don't tell him that I've already gone into horror movie mode, but he knows it.

My mind is racing, trying to come up with ways it will survive what it has perceived as a horror movie here.

We're not splitting up at this point. Not a chance. And there had better be a reason for the noise. Or we will be sleeping in shifts with the door barricaded.

"Suit yourself," he says as he picks up the pace to get this over with. I hate it when he trivializes my feelings like this.

There's a knife block on my way to the living room, and I stop and pull out one of the steak knives.

"Really, Blake?" Corbin says when he catches sight of it. "You're gonna slip in your wet socks and land on that."

"I know I heard something, and I don't feel safe anymore. Someone is in the house. I heard shuffling, too."

"Shuffling?" His ears perk up when I say that part.

We walk through the living room and head for the stairs. He glances nervously back. "Just don't accidentally stab me with that, okay?"

"Don't worry, I only stab people who don't take noises seriously," I joke.

There's a light switch at the bottom of the dark staircase. Corbin flicks it on, but nothing happens. "Bulb must be out," he announces, then heads up… like a man who has never seen even one horror movie in his entire life.

I wait at the bottom, watching him, but I really don't have much of a choice here. I either follow him up those dark stairs, or stay at the bottom by myself.

I grab the railing and head up, too.

CHAPTER 8

AUDREY
Three Years Ago

If you squint at the fern leaves draping down the sides of the wardrobe, you can see a tiny camera watching you.

Untrained eyes would only know it was there if they had a detector.

Missy's voice rings out from behind the plant. *"I love you for doing this, Audrey."* She squeals a little. *"I just want you to know that. I consider us closer now."*

I am supposed to say "I love you, too." It's what everyone who works for Missy says.

I don't say it.

"We're going to have to hurry," she continues. *"There's a bag by my desk. Tell him you were supposed to drive that out to Middleton Estates this evening, but you forgot. Tell him I'm probably going to kill you for forgetting because it was the one thing I told you to do before I left town. Or something like that. You'll figure it*

out. It's a present from me. I want to see his reaction, so make sure that part is right in front of the camera."

I realize I have stooped to a new low in life. I go to put the negligee on.

"No. No. I just checked the garage cameras. He's on his way up, almost here, and I really want to see him catching you changing into my clothes. Pretend like he interrupted you. I'd love to see his reaction there, too. But hurry. Find the bag. Oh, I'm just so thankful. Love you, love you, love you."

There it is again. "Love you, too," I mumble as I walk across the room where, sure enough, there's a large brown paper bag sitting at the back side of Missy's desk that I hadn't noticed before, not sure how I missed it. It's completely out of place in her office.

I snatch it up and hold it out to the camera. "This one?"

"Of course, that one. There aren't others. Just give it to him, okay?"

I set it on the floor with my clothes.

Believe it or not, I didn't wake up one day and think to myself that I wanted to sleep with my boss's husband. When Missy came to me with the idea, I think my jaw dropped to the floor.

"I know what you've been up to, Audrey," she'd said a week and a half ago when she called me into her office to chat. She was sitting at her desk in her peach Chanel jacket.

I didn't say anything.

It has always been my philosophy in life to exercise my Miranda Rights early, and shut the hell up until I've figured out what someone wants to hold against me.

She went on. "CJ told me you asked him to move a camera in the garage for you last week, right before Brenda's car was keyed. Joy's too."

She waited a beat to see if I'd say anything. When I didn't, she went on. "He said you encouraged him to break into my office."

"That's not true," I replied, because it wasn't.

He said he could do it. I asked him to show me. It took the man ten minutes to unlock her door using a paperclip. It was less than impressive, but at least I thought it meant we could trust each other.

Apparently not.

Missy took off her jacket and handed it out to me. "You even tried on my clothes."

I didn't reach for the jacket. Didn't say anything. Just sat and regretted trusting CJ.

Was I supposed to apologize? Was I losing my job? Should I throw CJ under the bus?

If he moved the camera, then he was the one who keyed the cars, Missy. Think about it.

She slipped the jacket back on and tossed her long blonde hair over it so it fell perfectly along its tailored shoulders. "CJ's obsessed with you. You probably noticed that. Poor guy only told me because he's obsessed with me, too. Now, I'm not upset about the jacket or the camera, and don't worry, I won't have you arrested," Missy said.

She paused to let that sink in. "I won't even talk to HR about this because I believe in second chances, and it has occurred to me that I haven't properly welcomed you to Lagdon Marketing. How silly of me. We're all friends here. Some closer than others, but we all love each other. Every one of us. Would you like to be one of my closest friends?"

"Yes, of course," I said, because that sounded better than getting fired.

"Good, I was looking for a go-getter of a friend. Like you." She sat forward, leaning across her desk, her eyes skimming the cheap fabric of my one good blouse. "Have you ever heard of May Pang?"

I hadn't.

She explained who she was, but I still googled the woman later. Apparently, Yoko Ono had requested May, her assistant, have an affair with John Lennon when their marriage hit a rough patch.

"I want you to be my May, and try to have an affair with Jordan. I'll just be honest. I think he's going to have an affair anyway, but if he does it in private, I won't know. I *want* to know. I need to document it. Have proof. Because if he has an affair, then he gets almost nothing in the pre-nup. And I can tell he's attracted to you."

That part I knew. He always jokes with me when he comes by the office. He's got the dad jokes down, even though he's only about ten years older than me. I think it comes with popping out kids in life. He also lingers in the doorway when I'm there. Touches my arm on the way out.

"I don't think that's true."

"No, no. A wife can always tell. You're very beautiful," she went on. "And I can also tell by the way you practically fuck my wedding picture every time I call you into my office that you find him attractive, too."

I shook my head no.

She leaned back in her chair. The chair I'd sat in about ten times before, eye-fucking that wedding photo all I wanted when I'd sneak in here by myself.

"I treat my friends so, so good," she said. "I think I see a promotion to the strategy team in your very near future if you agree to do this. You could be the fastest entry-level employee to get there."

"I don't know."

"What do you mean you don't know? We'll put a camera in my office. It'll be easy." Her voice was a little less best-friendy at that point. "And if you refuse, I will have to bring my concerns about you to HR, so you might as well do it, right? It's a great offer. You'd be crazy not to take it."

And that's how, a week and a half later, I find myself standing naked in Missy's office, in front of her picturesque window, goosebumps forming along my arms, because things get cold fast once the custodian turns down the heat.

I hear shoes squeaking along the floor outside the door, coming down the hall. I feel the tension coming from my new best friend on the other side of the camera.

The door opens and I pretend like I was searching through the closet. I turn around. "I'm not dressed," I say to the shadow standing in the doorway, like that's not obvious.

I wrap my arms around my middle as Jordan Lagdon enters the room.

CHAPTER 9

Jordan is what some people might call a "beta male." Alphas like to dominate. Betas like to be dominated. Or something like that. It's not like I've studied it.

But Jordan took his wife's last name when they got married. *So beta.*

He stays home with the kids. He jumps when she snaps.

And now, he only takes a tiny step into this dark room. I hear him swallow hard and cough under his breath.

I know Missy's secretly hoping he'll be outraged to see the young new hire looking through his wife's things. She wants to hear him demand that I put everything back and get the hell out.

He does not look outraged.

"I got your message," he says, a small smile forming along his lips. *"Get a babysitter. Come to Missy's office. Something about a surprise for me."*

I sent the exact message Missy told me to send. He closes the door behind him.

"Surprise," I say as I drop my arms from my middle.

I laugh a little at the way he stumbles across the room. His eyes obviously haven't adjusted to the darkness as well as mine have.

"I'm just a little worried there might be cameras," I say when he gets closer.

"Oh no. Missy hates cameras in private places." His eyes scan my body when he says that last part. He lets out a breathless chuckle. "And no one checks the other cameras around here."

He's dressed casually. Jeans and a black t-shirt that stretches along his pecs every time he moves an arm.

"I guess if there were cameras, I'd be fired by now," I say.

He takes a step toward me.

I turn back to the closet. "I've tried on everything. I can't decide what to wear." I pull the Chanel jacket off its hanger and slip it on. It barely covers my breasts. I can tell he notices.

He's looking at me with those eyes. Not quite the same way he's looking at Missy in that photo, but close. He's a gorgeous man. Tall. Dark. A dimple when he smiles.

"I'm going to have to ask you to remove my wife's clothes immediately," he says, stepping so close I smell his cologne.

It's almost like I can hear Missy behind me, even though she doesn't say anything. I know she's watching.

And the camera's a little off centered so she can't really see much right now either.

I pick up the grocery bag by my feet. "Sorry. Late delivery," I say, holding it out to him, killing the mood. "Missy gave me this to take over to your place in the hills. I guess it's a present. I can't believe I forgot. She's going to kill me."

It's like he's knocked out of a daze. "Uh, thank you." He tosses the bag onto the floor and steps in closer. It lands with a thud.

"Don't you want to see what's in it?"

"I know what's in it," he says. "Do you really want to talk about this right now?"

I don't. I want to wrap my legs around Mr. Soulful Eyes and show my new bestie why this was a bad idea. Then, get promoted for it.

But Missy was right. This guy is exactly who she thinks he is. He's going to cheat, and she should have proof, so he gets nothing.

I take a step into the middle of the room, where the camera can see us.

He reaches down and picks up the bag, unfolding the top. "Today is our dating anniversary. Missy and I *almost* had our first date at Marie Callender's seven years ago, and she likes to remind me about it."

He holds out the opened bag, and I peek inside. Sure enough, there's a frozen Marie Callender chocolate pie from the freezer section of Ralph's.

"She gets you frozen food for your anniversary?"

He sighs. "It's a long story. You sure you want to talk about this?"

I nod. "Every detail."

"I'll give you the short version, but I have to warn you, it's pretty boring stuff."

His smile is crooked now, and I wonder if he's rethinking everything here. He ought to be. "I was a struggling artist before I got married. Photography. Videography. You name it. I started working for Missy when she stopped doing the YouTube stuff and started doing all the marketing and training videos. Anyway, my friend encouraged me to go for it, right? Ask Missy out. *The Missy Lagdon.* He even loaned me money to do it, but not much."

He rests his back against the armoire, fiddling mindlessly with the top of the bag. "It took me weeks to get up the courage, and I about shit myself when she actually said yes. *Where do you take someone like Missy Lagdon?* Apparently not Marie Callendar's, because as soon as I pulled into the lot, she laughed for three minutes straight, then offered to buy me dinner if she could pick the place. We went somewhere French and expensive. She didn't even need a reservation because everyone accommodates Missy Lagdon."

He sets the bag back down again. This time, a little gentler. "But she still gets me a Marie Callendar pie every year on our dating anniversary. Our little joke, I guess."

I get the sense from him that the pie means more than just a joke. It might also be a yearly reminder from Missy that she is the reason they have a large house in the best part of Middleton Estates. She is the reason he was able to quit his job. Why they can travel the world whenever they want.

If it weren't for her, they'd have to eat frozen food from the supermarket.

I can't help but picture all the many times the guy came by the office with their two kids in tow to "surprise" Missy with a tofu banh mi sandwich or a kale smoothie. She's rarely there, and he always has the same reaction.

"No, no. I thought I told her we were coming. The boys and I were just on our way to the park, anyway. No biggie. Anyone else want this?"

And now, she's out of town for their dating anniversary.

I cup my hand over his ear and whisper. "Wanna do something crazy with that pie?"

He can't pick the bag up fast enough. "Like what?"

I take the bag from his hand and lead him over to Missy's desk.

On my way, I turn and slip off the Chanel jacket, tossing it on top of the wardrobe, right over the fern.

CHAPTER 10

BLAKE
Present Day

THE BOARDS CREAK UNDER OUR WEIGHT AS WE HEAD UP the dark stairs, which is the only sound in the house besides the wind.

"Where were you, anyway?" I ask. "Did you even go down to the car?"

I can tell he's surprised I noticed. He pauses at the top of the stairs and peers back at me from the corner of his eye, waiting for me to catch up.

He tries the light switch up there, but nothing happens. He is still standing in the dark.

"I saw tracks in the snow, leading around the back-yard. All around," I add.

He lets out a quick chuckle. "I decided to wait until

tomorrow to go down the hill, when it's light and a little warmer," he says. "I remembered there was one of those root cellars on the property, so I looked around for that first, just to see if I could find more supplies."

"And…?"

"It was locked, but I think I can get into it."

"Oh good. I hope there's food," I say. That has to be why he took the shovel. I flick on the flashlight part of my phone and scan the hall with it. "Because I didn't see a phone, so I don't know how we're going to call anyone for help."

"You're kidding." He turns to me. My flashlight casts weird shadows along his face.

"I didn't check everywhere, though."

There are two bedrooms up here. One just to the left of the stairs, and another one down the hall on the other side of the upstairs bathroom.

He points to the one on the left, then opens the door. "This is the best room. Queen-sized bed," he says, like we're just looking around for what bedroom to stay in.

I know he doesn't believe me about the noise. He thinks I'm just being paranoid. And maybe I am.

He hits the light switch, and my shoulders soften a little when the lamp actually flicks on.

He turns around and sees my face. "Stop worrying. We're going to be fine. We can always watch DVDs all weekend."

I shake my head. "We *could*… if the DVD player had a cord. But there's no power cord either…" I shrug. "So much for *Honey, I Shrunk the Kids* tonight."

He steps into the room. "Oh man, that would've been

a good one. We're finding that cord. It's gotta be in one of these rooms."

Corbin was right. This is a nice room. There's a blood-red bedspread with the large silhouette of a bear right in the middle, and about seven throw pillows placed along the headboard to make it look comfy. Like the downstairs, everything is accented in wood and bears, and sometimes a combination of both.

The plush dark brown carpet feels good under my socked feet, and there's even a portable heater in case things get too cold.

Corbin checks the drawers and closet while I lift the edge of the bedspread and peek under the bed.

There's nothing under there except a couple of old board games and some playing cards.

We leave the room and check the next one, which is similarly decorated and also similarly empty. No phone. No DVD cord. No food. But also no intruder, so there's always the positive.

And I start to feel my grip on the knife loosen. My fingers need a break. They've been clamped around this thing for far too long and everything aches.

I have no idea how serial killers do it. It is a lot of effort to maintain that position.

Corbin opens the last drawer in the second bedroom. It's full of extra blankets. "There's no way anyone but a housekeeper made any of these beds," he says as we leave the room.

I know he's just trying to get out of changing the sheets. But I do have to agree that both of the beds so far have the throw pillows facing the right way, and the bedspread designs perfectly lined up along the corners of the mattresses.

He opens the linen closet on our way to the bathroom. It's lined in more stiff white sheet sets, extra cleaner, and a vacuum.

"Still want me to change the sheets?" he asks.

"Yes," I say. "You're not getting out of that one."

He grunts like he can't believe it as we enter the upstairs bathroom, which is really small as far as bathrooms go. Toilet. Sink. No shower. No window.

But there's a small storage door on the wall by the toilet. We both notice it, I can tell.

We turn to each other. Without saying a word, Corbin cautiously approaches the door. It's a very short door that neither one of us could walk through without crouching down. I offer him my knife, but he shakes it off and puts his hand on the little knob.

He motions for me to get the knife ready, then opens the door and gasps loudly. "Ohmygod!"

I scream, until I realize he's using his joking voice. "Stop it. I could've cut something," I say, waving my knife a little in his direction. "Or someone."

We both peer into the closet, but it looks like there's really only about ten boxes of tile stacked in the space and some extra toilet paper.

He closes the door, and we go back out to the dark hallway.

I don't want to admit it to Corbin, but I'm starting to think the noise must have been my imagination, because nothing is broken or even out of place.

Maybe there is a ghost, just making random noises up here.

Or maybe I'm just feeling a little nervous tonight because this is my first real snowstorm, there's not much food, and I found a cryptic message in a guest book.

"Happy?" Corbin asks as he kisses my forehead.

I nod, even though I'm not.

"You hungry? Let's start heating the jacuzzi, and we'll look through all the cabinets downstairs, gather all of our supplies, and ration things out."

Ration things out.

He knows there's no way his friends are making it up. Otherwise, he'd have suggested we gorge ourselves on the salad and donuts I bought at the Olsen Mart.

And this worries me more than it should.

As we walk down the hall to go downstairs, I notice a cord dangling from the ceiling.

The attic.

I point my flashlight up to the rectangular opening in the ceiling. "We need to check that, too," I say.

He bites on the corner of his bottom lip and scrunches his face up. I can tell he does not want to go up there. I don't mention the guest book entries about rats and roaches. It's obviously better if I don't.

"If you check the attic, you don't have to make the beds," I say.

"You should have said that in the first place." He stands on his toes, grabs the tip of the pull cord and yanks it until the board in the ceiling creaks open on its hinge, revealing a foldable ladder attached to the underside of the board.

Corbin mutters that he can't believe the things I talk him into doing (like it's a lot) then straightens out the ladder.

He rests his foot on the first rung, slowly putting all his weight on it, checking to make sure it's sturdy enough. The light from his phone flickers around the hallway, and I fully expect to see a rat jump out from one of the rooms and into the beam.

"Maybe changing the sheets isn't so bad, after all," he says, like checking the attic is optional at this point.

"Just go," I say. "I heard a noise, and I'm not going to be able to sleep until we figure out what made it."

He climbs up the ladder, and I make sure I've got a good grip on the knife, even though I'm not sure what I'd do if he actually called out for help.

Would I really climb this rickety ladder in my boyfriend's huge jacket, carrying a steak knife to save the day?

Can steak knives even save the day?

Eventually, he's at the top, poking his head into the darkness of the attic.

"You better not try to scare me again," I call up to him as he hoists himself into the space itself. And before I know it, I'm standing in the dark hallway by myself.

I wasn't expecting him to actually go in there. I thought he'd just *look* around.

His footsteps echo down on me, like he's stomping around. Something slides across the floor. Something closes, followed by the sound of something else dropping.

And the noises sound a lot like the noise I heard earlier.

"Everything okay?" I yell up to him. "What do you see?"

He doesn't answer.

I let out a shaky breath. A part of me knows he *wants* me to go up, so he can try to scare me again. He does that a lot, not sure why.

"Corbin?" I call up again.

Still no answer.

I tuck my phone into my back pocket and take off his jacket so it doesn't get in the way, tossing it onto the floor. Then, I grab the ladder with my left hand, making sure I have a good solid hold before climbing up, taking each step slowly because a girl in wet socks carrying a steak knife up a rickety ladder really can't be too careful in life.

Especially since a trip to the ER is going to be out of the question tonight. And I'd like to come out of this with all of my toes.

"I swear to God, if you jump out when I get to the top, I will cut you. And no jury will convict me for doing it."

I suddenly realize *that's exactly how someone would joke in a horror movie...*

CHAPTER 11

The attic is darker than I thought it'd be. The tiny light-bulb hanging from the ceiling doesn't do much, and neither does the flashlight from Corbin's cellphone that has been positioned so it acts more like a lantern.

At first, I don't even see my boyfriend because it's *that* dark, but then I notice his tall frame standing at the window, tugging on it.

He's the only one up here, thank God.

I rest my knife on the attic floor and hoist myself into the space itself. It's dusty and cold up here, even colder than the rest of the house, like heat has never reached this part, ever. My feet feel like ice cubes, and I regret leaving Corbin's jacket in the hall downstairs.

My boyfriend turns when he hears me. "Good news and bad news," he says.

His face is ghostly white. His blonde hair sticks up in weird spots, like he's been running his hand over his head a million times. "This window was left open."

"Is that the good news or the bad news?"

"It's both. The good news is I'm sure a gust of wind knocked this old lamp off that dresser, so that's the noise you heard." He points to a ceramic lamp on the floor by some stuffed animals. It's pretty much shattered.

"But the bad news is, the window doesn't seem to close all the way," he adds. "And it's pretty windy."

It's one of those crank-out windows, and he spins the crank to show it no longer works. The window is partially open.

"No wonder it's so cold up here," I say.

"I think someone has to push on the backside to get it to close all the way." He reaches his hand around the pane and tugs. It hardly budges.

I look around to see if there's a way to rig the thing shut while we're here, realizing just how strange the attic is.

There's a chest of drawers, and a wooden rocking chair in the corner. Barbies and stuffed animals have been lined up along the back wall like they're watching us. There are also a couple of Furbies and some Cabbage Patch dolls.

It kind of seems like a child's playroom from the 90s, if children played in dark attics. My eyes scan the floorboards for rat droppings or movement.

I make my way over to the dresser, where the pieces of lamp are scattered around, and open the top drawer. There are clothes in there. Shirts. Sweaters. Snow hats. And more cracker crumbs. I open the next drawer down, noticing a lump of cords. I tug them out, and a small white video monitor falls to the floor with a thud.

"Do you think someone could be living up here?" I ask. "Climbing in and out through the window. Knowing when people are here by using this video monitor." I hold it up. It's old and clunky and probably hasn't been used in thirty years.

I know I sound ridiculous as soon as the words leave my mouth.

"So, you think someone is living in a freezing cold attic… to do what?" He motions around. "Play Barbies? Steal DVD cords and phone books?"

"I'm just saying I don't know if I'm going to be able to sleep tonight. Not in this house."

My eyes do not leave the creepy doll party along the wall.

"Where are you going to sleep then, Blake? A hotel? The car?"

He wraps an arm around my shoulder. "If it will make you feel any better, we'll figure out a way to lock this window up, then we'll binge on the food you bought at the mini-mart. I'm sure I'll be able to get into the cellar tomorrow. There's probably a ton of canned stuff in there."

"What if you get in there, and there's nothing?"

"My friends will be here…" He stops talking. I can tell he knows where I'm going with this. The stores are all closed. The snowplow isn't even coming for a while. And his friends are all at home in Middleton.

"Okay, maybe we shouldn't *binge* on all the food tonight," he says. "But I still have part of a sandwich left in the car, and there's definitely champagne and beer in there."

I don't ask if the sandwich will still be good if we leave it in the car overnight. The car is a freezer right now.

Everything is a freezer, including this attic.

He takes the mound of cords from me. "Now let's see if any of these are the elusive power cord we need for the DVD player."

He starts to untwist the tangled mess, pulling cords out from their knot, but it quickly becomes apparent they're mostly just extension cords. He stuffs them back in the drawer and we check the place over for anything useful.

As he peeks in more drawers, I look out the window at the night.

I only see the same tracks I saw before, all around the backyard, and into the side yard where the attic window faces, but even those tracks are quickly fading from the new-fallen snow.

I now know they were Corbin's footprints, as he searched for food and supplies, trying to get into the cellar, wherever that is.

He probably didn't want me to know just how dire our situation is here. He always tries to protect me.

Just as I turn away from the glass, I notice there's a tree by the side of the house, with branches extending out to the opened window. In fact, I could literally reach my hand out of the little opening and touch one of the biggest branches if I wanted to.

And a part of me wants to do it, because the branch doesn't have snow on it like some of the others, and I want to see just how sturdy it is.

"I think someone climbed that tree," I say, pointing to the branch.

Corbin lets out a loud sigh. "I saw the tree and thought of that. But I don't think it's possible. Plus, it would be crazy to climb a tree in a snowstorm."

I rub my hands over my sweatshirt, but I'm still shivering.

"You should go downstairs where it's warmer. Grab my jacket again," he says.

I shake my head no. "Not until we get that window rigged shut."

"Okay, okay." He looks around the room and points to the dresser. "Help me move that over."

He grabs one of the teddy bears propped against the wall and sets it on top of the dresser. "If we move this next to the window, we can use it to rig the thing closed."

I don't question it. I just grab one end of the dresser while he grabs the other. The thing doesn't slide as easily as I was hoping. It's much heavier than it looks, and it makes an eerie screeching sound as it partially drags over the floorboards. Eventually, we have it in the spot he was directing us to.

He takes the scarf off the teddy bear and knots one end of it around the crank and the other around the knob of the dresser until it's as tight as he can get it.

"If anyone did climb the tree before, they won't be able to tug the window open now," he says, looking out at the snow again.

He wraps an arm around my shoulders and pulls me in for a hug. "Happy?"

I am far from happy. I feel more like a prisoner in this place. Afraid to stay. Unable to leave.

I am trapped.

He presses his cheek over mine. "You're so cold. Come on, let's go downstairs. I know this isn't ideal, but I *did* find some firewood in the shed. And plenty of it. I'll make a fire. A big one. And if you want, you can take the whole block of knives and all the food and sit right in front of the fire while I check the house over for the phone and the cord for the DVD player. I'm going to try getting into the cellar again, too, because I promised you food, and I'm going to deliver."

My stomach rumbles when he says the part about the food.

"So eat as much as you want. You were the one who bought all the food at our last stop."

"I'm not doing that. We're going to ration it out." I smile at him, and he leans in to kiss me.

Corbin always knows exactly what to say to make me feel better about things. And it does make sense to warm up by a fire and relax. Plus, I want to look through that guest book a little more without him around.

On my way out, I look back at the window, trying not to picture a hand, tugging that scarf loop off.

CHAPTER 12

Leave it to my boyfriend to come up with the best plan ever.

I'm sitting directly on the raised hearth, my back resting against the bricks just to the side of the fireplace opening itself.

How Corbin managed to make such a huge fire in under five minutes is something I will never understand. I know his mom used to take him to Boy Scouts before she died when he was young.

But this is some wizardry stuff.

It's strange how little he talks about his mom, or his dad, a man I have never even met. Apparently, he's some sort of socially awkward hermit who got even more socially awkward after Corbin's mom died. He doesn't meet people, which explains a lot about Corbin, honestly. It must have been hard to grow up that way.

The heat is a little too much, even for me. I have to switch sides every once in a while as I curl up in the scratchy crochet throw, with my laptop on my lap and the knife block beside me.

The metal bin by the fireplace has been filled to the brim with logs now. Corbin told me to keep the fire going. *"Just add a log every ten minutes or so."*

The house is locked up. The heat has kicked in.

I should feel safe and secure, but I don't.

The front door is just to my left, the dark stairs to the left of that, and I can't stop looking over at them, expecting another noise or a shadow.

I jokingly told Corbin I would "get dinner ready" while he looked for supplies. Like we thought, there was nothing in the house, so he's gone back out to try the cellar again.

But, when I rationed things out for tonight, I realized just how sad our dinner actually is.

From what I can tell, there are about 100 Pringles in the can, give or take a few, so I think we're safe to eat ten a day each, and a small handful of trail mix.

He thinks the storm will let up soon, but we can't count on it. So that is about all we should eat tonight.

Even on the smallest plates in the cupboard, "dinner" still looks like less than you'd give a rabbit.

I put everything on the coffee table about ten minutes ago before I sat down. But I swear to God, if I look over and there's a rat sitting up there, chowing down on our rations, I will run onto the porch again.

I'm sure Corbin would laugh and say something weird like, "We should catch it in case things get too dire. So we can cook it up."

Because he thinks grossing me out is funny. He always does.

When we first started dating, he used to point out road kill to me because he knew it made me squirm, saying stuff like, "There's a good one, Blake. Look at that."

I actually had to have a serious talk with him about what was an acceptable joke and what crossed the line. It was part of the reason my oldest brother asked if I was Corbin's first girlfriend.

And sure, he is quirky, but we're working on boundaries, and he always has my back.

I open the old clothbound guest book again. The thin, grayish stationery paper falls out, and I unfold it.

IFIDISAPPE

I turn and open the fireplace screen, tossing the message on the top log, watching as it burns to nothing.

Then, I bring up a new Word document on my laptop, and type in the message there, turning off auto-correct.

I pick up where I left off.

IFIDISAPPEAR

There are more letters underlined in the subsequent pages, but things are already thinning out.

I'm at 2006 where a family from San Francisco was glad their cousin had turned them onto this place.

"I've never been to a ski resort that wasn't crowded before. How do they stay in business?"

I'm only looking for the underlined letters now. And only the ones underlined with one line, not two.

It takes me some time to get the hang of it again. I

can't miss an underlined letter, or it throws the message off, and I have to go back through the whole thing and figure out where I went wrong, which is hard because there are no spaces in the message.

I have to be quick. Corbin will be returning from the cellar soon.

It's not long before a second message forms in my Word document.

MYNAMEISAUDR

I can't finish the message fast enough. It's exactly what I thought it'd be.

MYNAMEISAUDREYRANDALL

I kind of knew who the author was. I had a feeling it was her. It had to be her.

How many other people went missing around here?

Hopefully not many.

But yet, as I stare at the message, I think it could also be someone's idea of a joke. This cabin is very close to the old mill and the ski resort where she was last spotted.

So someone could've thought it'd be funny to put a message in the guest book after seeing her missing-person poster.

It's a slim-to-none possibility, but one I still need to consider.

Why didn't Corbin tell me his friend owned the cabin that Audrey had disappeared from when I brought out her poster in the car?

I look over at the skis propped along the back wall of the stair landing — lonely and dark — and inch closer to the fire.

My muscles tighten because the feeling is back. Like

something bad is about to happen, and I can't get warm enough.

He should have told me at that point. I need to ask him…

I hunch over my laptop protectively and continue on. Like everything else in life, there's got to be a logical explanation, I know it. I'm being silly.

I don't see anything on the next page, so I skip it and go onto the one after that where there are more lines. A lot more.

UPSTASBT

Something seems off. It's not forming a word like it should be. I start over and go slower. It's very easy to miss a line.

UPSTAIRSBATHROOMSTORAGE

That's the end of the messages underlined with one line. Audrey left something in the storage area of the bathroom upstairs.

I snap the guest book closed along with my laptop, and tuck them both inside my backpack next to the knife that's already in there, and zip them all up.

Then I open the metal bin and tug out another log, gently placing it on top of the other logs so the fire won't die while I'm upstairs.

For some reason, I don't want Corbin to know what I'm doing. And that log will buy me a good ten minutes or so.

CHAPTER 13

AUDREY
Three Years Ago

Joy glances up from the Keurig as I pass the coffee break area and hurry over to my desk Monday morning. I feel like the whole place knows what Jordan and I did in Missy's office Friday night with the pie.

I have no idea what to expect now. I definitely messed up.

And the worst part of any mess-up is always the clean up that happens afterwards. I'm not just talking about Missy's office when Jordan and I finished on the floor in front of the main window.

As you can imagine, that was a disaster.

I'll never forget how he turned and wiped chocolate cream from my hair. "I hate to leave you with this…" he whispered, motioning around the office.

Pie was everywhere. On the floor by the window. On Missy's chair and the desk.

"But I have kids and a babysitter. You understand, right?"

"Oh yeah, I get it," I whispered back, like I actually did.

We were using his t-shirt as a blanket. I pulled it up, so it covered our faces when we talked, muffling our whispered voices for the camera, in case Missy was still listening in or recording. "Good thing Missy has a private bathroom."

He chuckled. "Yeah, good thing. Shouldn't be too hard for either one of us to clean up. You're wonderful. You know that, right?" He squeezed my shoulders, tickling the side of my arm with his thumb, but his eyes scanned the room from the side of the t-shirt. "You sure you don't mind?"

Yes, Jordan. I mind. This is a shit ton of work to clean up. And it's not exactly something I can leave for the custodian.

I wiggled myself against the warmth of his bare chest. "No. Go ahead."

It was my own fault, really. I'd felt sorry for the man. And I lost all track of what I was supposed to be doing for my new best friend.

"I'll make it up to you," he said. "Missy's going to LA on Wednesday. Come by our house after work. I'll make you my famous soufflé that Missy won't touch anymore after she went vegan because… you know, eggs." He tugged the t-shirt from my grasp. "Sorry, I have to take this."

I watched him scoop up his pants and head into Missy's bathroom to freshen up.

I had no idea if I should tell Missy about my invitation for Wednesday or not. I probably shouldn't go.

I should just pretend I had no idea I messed up, and tell her about the invitation for Wednesday.

It's all I can think about now, as Joy follows me through the maze of desks, blowing on her million-dollar coffee, acting like she knows everything. She *is* Missy's friend, so she *could* know. I somehow doubt it. "What'd you do this weekend? You have the notes ready for the big meeting, right? All of them."

"Of course," I say, and I do. I spent most of the weekend sitting in front of my laptop at my kitchen table, googling "How to do market research…"

I don't know why I bothered. I'm about to lose my job, anyway. Missy won't be in until after lunch, so maybe I won't lose my job until then.

"Missy can't make the meeting," Joy says as she sips her coffee. "She's stuck on the East Coast. All flights were canceled because of the weather, and I guess she doesn't have time for a Zoom, so we're having the meeting early."

I let out a shaky laugh. She's not here. I don't have to face her.

"Do you mind if I peek at your notes? I could give you a few pointers," she says when I sit down at my desk and turn on my laptop. "You probably don't need help, though. UCLA. Magna cum laude. Or was it summa? My God. I'm a state school girl myself."

"I don't think it matters where you graduate."

The crinkles around her 30-year-old eyes always

deepen when she smiles. "You're probably right. Just that you actually *do graduate*." She leans over my desk. "I don't know if I told you this, but I have a friend who went to UCLA at the same time you did. Communications major, too. Small world, right?"

She looks up and sees CJ and Ryan making their way around the desks. "We'll talk more later," she says and moves on.

CJ is carrying two specialty coffees from the snack cart in the lobby. I know one is for me because I told him I hate coffee-pod coffee, so he's been buying me a different coffee to try every Monday since.

I quickly open a tab on my laptop to bring up my email and pretend not to see them. I haven't talked to CJ since he threw me under the bus with Missy almost two weeks ago. He keeps trying. Keeps bringing me coffee.

He stops at my desk. "It's a fun one today. The barista downstairs assures me this is her new favorite. Some fancy java chip thing…"

I barely look over at him. "No thanks," I say.

He stands there. So much passes between us. *Yes, CJ, I did find out you told Missy how we went into her office. How I asked you to move a camera.*

He sets the cup on the edge of my desk. "I'll leave it here, if you change your mind. Mondays are hard." He's so close his hip brushes the side of my shoulder. I do not look up at him and smile coyly like I used to. We are not sharing a joke about Mondays. Or coffee. Or anything.

"I'm not going to change my mind. Just take it," I say.

"I only bought it…" His voice rises.

"Do you want me to pay you back?" This time, I turn sharply toward him.

Out of the corner of my eye, I see Ryan, holding in a laugh.

CJ tugs on a strand of hair. "It feels like you're mad at me."

"I'm not." I say it so quickly, nobody would be confused by the connotation. If I were a text, I'd be in all-caps right now. I *AM* mad. We *ARE* done.

Ryan backs away, but CJ doesn't.

He playfully bumps my shoulder again. "Oh thank God," he says, with a strange kind of laugh as he scoops the coffee from off my desk. "Some days I don't want coffee either. Messes with my stomach. I guess I'll just find someone else who wants this today."

"You found one," Ryan says, grabbing the cup from CJ. "Thanks, bruh."

CJ looks at me. His eyes beg for forgiveness. But I look away, searching through my email instead because forgiveness is not happening. I am not someone who gives out second chances.

There are a ton of new messages this morning. It's funny how they accumulate. Lagdon Marketing doesn't work with everyone, and so many people see me as a gate-keeper to Missy. I will be spending my morning being young and cheerful as I reply back, using variations on the script I've been given.

Joy watches me from across the office as she talks to Brenda. Only she doesn't want me to know. Every time I look over, she turns so quickly her strawberry blonde "influencer-curled" hair falls along the side of her face. I wonder if they're still talking about how their cars were keyed a couple of weeks ago.

Come on, ladies. Make the connection here. Fuck with me and you'll get fucked with.

Joy's eyes widen, and her face goes from rosy to sickly pale in about a second. She cups a hand over her mouth and runs, hunched over, across the office to the restroom in the hall.

I see her coffee's kicked in.

I turn back to the emails, noticing at the last second that one stands out because it's been labeled "URGENT: OPEN NOW" in all caps. *All caps.*

It's from Missy.

I wait to click on it until I'm sure Ryan and CJ are back at their desks, minding their own problems, and I am alone.

CHAPTER 14

There is no way I can ignore this email, even though I really want to pretend I don't see it.

Looks like I really did mess up. Again.

I should not have thrown the jacket on top of the camera. I should not have agreed to be in that room in the first place.

Did I even clean it up enough? Who knows?

I pride myself on staying on top of things. On being one step ahead of everyone else, on making a plan and sticking to it. Then I let my emotions get in the way and make a rash decision.

Story of my life.

I am a woman about to get fired, or at least, investigated by HR, whatever that means.

CJ is halfway sitting on Ryan's desk. They're both looking at Ryan's laptop. He smiles when he catches my eye and runs a hand through his greasy blonde hair, allowing his bangs to fall bit by bit back onto his large forehead. He knows something.

Would Missy have told the rest of the office before telling me?

"You know what this means, right?" he yells to me, pointing at his computer screen. He doesn't wait for me to answer. "We're taking you out to lunch. Lagdon Marketing tradition. Our treat."

Going out to lunch with that guy is the last thing I want to do on my last day.

I click on the email.

Congratulations, Audrey!!! You're now a member of the strategy team. I'll let everyone know first thing Monday morning.

 XX,
 Missy

And just like that, I suddenly feel about six steps behind on everything.

CHAPTER 15

I've never wondered what hell was like before. Even when I was 13 years old, being forced to study the Bible, I couldn't picture it.

But if I had to guess, the last ten minutes of polite conversation at Stucky's Bar and Grill would have to come close.

"C'mon, Audrey, tell us your secrets. No other entry-level's made it this fast. It took me a full year."

"Who did you sleep with?"

"Did you bribe someone?"

I'm just thankful not everyone from the strategy team was able to make it to my welcome-aboard lunch, like Joy, who was too sick to come.

My arms are glued tightly across my chest as I shrink down in our tiny booth, which only amplifies the noises around me.

Laughter from the other tables. Clinking glasses. Women in tailored skirts with stuffy buns throwing their heads back, relishing the sound of their own jokes. Men in designer button-downs, passing around their phones. Probably some sort of meme about stocks. Who knows?

I've never seen the lunch crowd around work before.

Ryan told me I'd love the vibe.

I think I'd rather take a paper cut to the eyeball.

Thank God Lagdon Marketing is picking up the tab. Burgers cost more than I paid for my entire outfit, but I quickly see why Missy allows it. Just having her employees be seen in this place is the real attraction here. It is easily the place to be in downtown on any given weekday. But I'm not noticing the view.

The afternoon light streaming in from the window by our side spotlights the lines in Brenda's scowl.

To be fair, Brenda's always scowling. It might not be me this time. She's the 40-something at work frustrated by all the young people having fun.

She sits up straighter when I shrink farther. "It was clearly something in her presentations," she says to everyone else because she rarely talks directly to me. She grabs another chip and swirls it around the small bowl of salsa. "I particularly loved the part this afternoon when marketing strategies were explained to us via PowerPoint."

We all know my presentations are straight from Google. I add nothing of value to this table.

But I'm not going to let it show.

"I don't know why I got promoted, you guys," I finally say, sitting up again. "Missy told me once that I reminded her of herself when she was my age." It's true. She did say that at my interview. "She also told me she loves my go-getting attitude." Also true. But she said that right before asking me to be the next May Pang.

The waitress sets a round of margaritas in front of us that Ryan talked us into ordering because "we can just take a late lunch today."

I've never worked at a place where you can drink at lunch. Or fudge when you came back.

But we're all friends at Lagdon Marketing. Apparently.

Ryan raises his glass. "To Audrey, the new go-getting Missy Lagdon," he says, and we all cheers.

"And don't worry," CJ says as he pulls the little basket of chips closer to our side of the table. "I can help you. But it's easier than it looks, anyway. Easy as pie," he adds, cupping his hand over mine.

I quickly stand and make him get up so I can head to the bathroom.

There is no way he knows about the pie. And who cares if he does?

I push open the restroom door, but I don't go in a stall. I head straight to the sink and splash a little water on my face, staring at myself in the mirror, running a finger over my eyeliner, fixing my tucked in blouse.

Nothing makes sense.

I messed up Friday night. Big time. Why on earth have I been promoted? And what does being on the strategy team even mean?

I glance around at the ocean blue accents and the trendy mural painted directly on the wall behind me. A decorative map of Middleton.

The move here was supposed to be my fresh start. I pretty much pawned my entire existence for the chance to become something I always knew I could be, if I was given the chances everyone else was given in life.

And being promoted is step one. I should feel lucky here. But also, cautious. Because if anyone knows there's no such thing as luck, it's the girl who also knows there's no such thing as karma.

You have to create that stuff on your own.

A woman enters the restroom, knocking me back to reality. I grab a couple of paper towels, dry my hands, and leave.

At least a plan is forming in my head now to figure this out. Maybe I'll accept Jordan's invitation, after all.

Lunch is waiting for me at the table when I get back. A hamburger with a little colorful toothpick sticking out of its bun to fancy it up.

Because that's all that separates a $6 burger from a $55 one, when you think about it. You just gotta look the part. Act the part. Declare that your weird herbs and toasted bun mean you are worth the markup.

"I might be able to join you guys this time," Brenda says as I slide into my spot at the booth. She sets her napkin down and stands, excusing herself to the restroom.

It's not lost on me that the woman waited until I came back to go herself. She wants me to know we are not friends.

She blames me for her keyed car. I know it.

"I'm not going if she goes," CJ says once Brenda's out of earshot. "Last time, she spent half the night lecturing us on being quiet after 10:00."

"It's your own fault for bringing it up. It'll be fine.

We'll invite a bunch of young people, so maybe she won't want to go. All the usuals. Tyler… Ben," Ryan says, taking a bite of his chicken sandwich.

"Or Audrey," CJ adds. His eyes meet mine, but I glare at him and grab the ketchup bottle.

He doesn't seem to notice anything strange between us. "Brenda definitely won't go if Audrey goes. She hates you, Audrey."

He turns to me, laughing like he thinks I will find that funny. "You should have heard her when you were in the bathroom…"

I squeeze the ketchup bottle harder. A large glob forms on my plate next to the crinkle fries.

"Really, bruh?" Ryan interrupts, shaking his head at CJ. His dark brown hair falls into his eyes, and he brushes it away and smiles at me. "Brenda doesn't hate you. And we're all going skiing at this awesome cabin, if you want to come."

And in that moment, I see why Joy still pines for this guy. He's a little short, but he's very handsome, dimple in his chin, nice clothes. Plus, there's just something about him that puts you at ease.

"What'd Brenda say when I was in the bathroom?" I ask.

It's not like I don't know who that woman is in life. I overheard her and Joy conspiring to get me fired once. Nothing on paper, nothing I could prove. But I've had to make a presentation at every meeting since.

Ryan motions with a french fry. "Oh, you know… just regular office gossip. She doesn't think you're ready, that's all." He glances at the bathroom area.

"You can tell me later," I say, scooting closer to him. "I was actually hoping to pick your brain about the strategy team and my new promotion, anyway."

"I'd love to help," CJ chimes in, but I don't even turn in his direction. I see him out of the corner of my eye, though. Shifting in his seat. His face growing red.

Ryan leans back and smiles. "I've never *mentored* anyone before, but I guess I could."

"Great," I say. "It might be confusing for me to have too much help," I add, as my eyes finally meet CJ's.

But his aren't caring and soft like I expect them to be. They don't beg me for forgiveness anymore. They're distant. Cold. I'm not even sure he's seeing me.

I look away and pull the toothpick out of my $55 burger.

CHAPTER 16

BLAKE
Present Day

The tile floor in the upstairs bathroom feels like ice. I half-listen for noises as I rest my back against the scratchy towel hanging off the rack behind me.

Usually, germs are a huge concern. Corbin gets on my nerves with how he can eat anything, anywhere, without washing his hands or using hand sanitizer.

But sitting on a bathroom floor is the least of my worries.

Just outside the door to my right is the hallway where the attic entrance is located. And the window that doesn't lock or even close all the way.

There's also no heat in this bathroom, so I'd like to figure this out quick and get back to the fire. I pull down the towel and drape it over my shoulders.

Audrey's message said something about the upstairs

bathroom storage, but Corbin and I already checked that area, and there wasn't anything in there but boxes of old floor tile and some bulk toilet paper.

The guest book is open on my lap, my laptop next to me. I've finished the message underlined once, so I go back to the beginning entries and start on the letters underlined twice.

DRAOBDEKR

I take my time, checking each one, but I have to be missing something.

The words look like gibberish. Maybe this *is* a sick joke, after all.

I grab my cellphone. It's 11:17 and my eyes are burning. Corbin's been gone forty-five minutes.

At what point do I worry about him?

It's not now. Because I don't want him here. I finish writing the second message, and just like I thought, the whole thing doesn't make sense.

DRAOBDEKRAMLLAWTFEL

My heart beats faster, picturing Corbin coming into the living room and not seeing me at the fire. Picturing a scared Audrey three years ago, frantically putting her code in this book so whoever she was with wouldn't know she was doing it.

She probably didn't have much time to come up with any other plan.

So, if this is some sort of word scramble, it's probably an easy one.

I look over at the small, off-centered door that leads to the storage area. I've got to hurry. The time to do this is now.

I've been in this bathroom for more than ten minutes already. I'm going to have to add another log to the fire soon.

I stand to do that, noticing my laptop's screen in the mirror.

I cock my head to the side and blink at the message on my bright white Word document. The puzzle *was* simple. I was just panicking. Corbin was right. Nothing ever works right when you're panicking.

I just needed to look at the thing backwards.

LEFTWALLMARKEDBOARD

CHAPTER 17

I toss the towel onto the floor by the cabinet.

But instead of heading into the closet, I turn and open the bathroom door, taking a few steps into the hall, listening for any sign that Corbin is already downstairs. Or anyone is above me in the attic.

I don't hear anything. I close and lock the door again, then make my way to the storage door by the toilet, yanking it open.

A cold draft sweeps over me, like a ghost, if I believed in those.

I hunch down and step around the tile boxes and toilet paper, careful not to knock over anything.

Heading left. My only direction.

I flick on my phone's flashlight and shine it around the entire place.

None of the walls are finished on the inside of the closet, and I see in the distance that the place thins out in the back. The already-short ceiling grows shorter and shorter until you'd have to be an animal to get back there.

I try not to think about small animals being back there.

As soon as I'm safely past the boxes, I sit down and inspect the boards along the left wall. I make a plan to scan every one of them, bottom to top, as I search for some sort of marking. Not sure what.

The light from the bathroom helps a little. And even though I want to find the marked board now, I know I can always come back and look if I don't see it by the time Corbin gets back.

It might be easier in the light of day, even though this bathroom doesn't get much light.

I'll just tell him I have an upset stomach if he asks why I'm spending so much time in here.

The unfinished boards have all been stamped with markings from whatever lumber yard or store they were purchased from when these walls were created, but that can't be the markings I'm looking for.

I stand up, as much as I can, to check the top side by the ceiling, but I have to jut my neck out at a weird angle when I do it. I don't like being here, hunched over, in this closet. It's weird and dark. There are cobwebs every-where, and God knows what else. I try to inhale, but I can't breathe deeply. All I suck in is stale dust.

I shake off the feelings of claustrophobia that being in a closet brings. I can't imagine Audrey liked it much, either.

She'd probably have made this quick. So this must be more obvious than I'm making it here.

I move a few inches over to check the next set of boards, starting at the top, shining my light over everything. The faded markings in the guest book were all made in pencil, so I might be looking for something very faint.

Squishy pink insulation fills the spots between the boards along the left wall. I take a deep breath and shove my hand into the cotton-like material, feeling for anything out of the ordinary, hoping the stuff isn't asbestos.

What does asbestos feel like?

I take my hand out again and run a finger over the boards themselves, while illuminating every spot, taking it inch by inch. A splinter shoots into my forefinger.

But I just keep going.

I've almost made my way to the farthest part of the closet, checking over the boards near the floor, when I finally see it. Three faded Xs that I would never have noticed if I hadn't known to look for them. If I hadn't been checking every inch. My heart leaps into my throat.

I give it a little tug. But it's just a normal board, not loose or anything.

I scan the area around it for another message, another clue. But there's nothing. I shove my hand into the insulation itself, checking on the other side of the marked board, and that's when I feel the very edge of something hard.

I pick at it a little with my thumb and forefinger, but I can't quite grab it.

I pull my hand out and try it from a different angle because whatever it is has been wedged securely behind this board, covered by the insulation. And the thing is smooth and hard to grip…

What is it?

Sweat pools along my hairline, despite it being ice cold in here, as I pinch my fingers around the tip of the object, trying to wiggle it free.

I don't have much time. I need to hurry. I shake my hands out, determined to get it. The thought that I might need to go downstairs and grab a butter knife horrifies me.

I really don't want to do that.

I pinch my fingers around the wedged object one last time. This time I'm able to grip a couple of fingernails firmly around its side. The thing starts to move, I can tell.

I give it a big tug, and I hear the sound of cracking and crunching. My fingers slip and I fall over with a thud. But the thing moved a lot that time.

I get back up and continue rocking and scraping the object up the board a half inch at a time. My breath is heavy now. It's all I can hear until I hear something else.

I stop dead in my tracks.

It's the sound of shaking.

Someone is trying to turn the bathroom knob.

CHAPTER 18

AUDREY
Three Years Ago

Jordan's arm is a dead weight on my neck. I lift it off and roll over, sliding my legs to the side of the bed so I don't wake him.

We're in the guest bedroom at his house in Middleton Estates. Missy's out of town. The kids are at a babysitter's.

The night with the soufflés has come and gone.

I actually let him clean that shit up himself that night after he knocked everything off the kitchen island in a fit of passion, straight out of a movie.

Right before that, he handed me a brown paper bag, just like I had that night in Missy's office. "Just a small surprise."

"This better not be pie," I said as I unfolded the opening. It wasn't. But it also wasn't jewelry, like I was hoping.

"A phone?"

"Untraceable," he explained, kissing my forehead gently. "It means I'm hoping to see you again and again. I enrolled the boys in daycare, too. But don't tell Missy."

He only told me that because he wants to sneak in a few lunchtime dates.

He doesn't know there is no chance I will tell Missy, because Missy and I do not talk anymore.

I get up. The bed creaks under my weight. I freeze and turn back around, checking that Jordan's eyes are still shut. They are.

I'd be surprised if they weren't.

I gave him a pretty large dose of sleeping pills about an hour ago, so I don't think he'll be waking up anytime soon, but there's always a chance.

I slip on the guest robe hanging on the back of the door and take a second to admire the man before I leave.

With the way the sheet drapes over his chiseled chest, he looks like one of those Greek god statues lying there in toga. Peaceful. Not a care in the world.

He's the type of person that everything always works out for in life. And I am his polar opposite.

I walk out of the room. The feeling of freedom surges over me. Possibilities. What should I look through? Fuck with? Try on?

I head down the hall and push open the door to Missy and Jordan's master suite. It's the biggest room I have ever seen.

Couches and a TV the size of a small sedan. A portrait of Missy hangs above the bed. She's naked, but strategically covered in rose petals. I've already checked the painting over, so I know it's just a painting — no cameras. No cameras anywhere, which is nice.

Jordan told me once that she doesn't want them around because she can't be herself when cameras are there. It's like a switch goes on in her mind whenever she knows she's being filmed. She turns into "influencer Missy." Charming Missy. Missy, the YouTube content creator.

My naked boss' eyes watch me from the painting, and I almost want to turn the thing over so she can't do it.

What kind of narcissist has that hanging over her bed?

I've only been in this room twice before. I like to take things methodically, and now, I'm on one of the walk-in closets.

I swing the closet door wide open. The smell of expensive perfume greets me as I flick on the light.

If I had more time, I'd try on a few of these outfits. That Louis Vuitton blouse looks like cake on a hanger, but I don't let myself even touch it.

Funny thing is, I don't see any men's clothing here. This whole closet must belong to Missy. Shoes and purses at the back. Work outfits at the front. Even a small vanity with a hairbrush and powder puff.

What in the actual hell?

A couple of dresses hang covered in cloth bags, and the 13-year-old in me wants to unzip them and peek inside to see what the cool girls get to wear in life.

Next time, I tell myself. I've got to find the good stuff now.

And I know the good stuff is never in plain sight. I run my hand against the back wall, inching my way along the smooth, cold drywall until I feel something rough and leathery.

I part the clothes away from the spot so I can see what it is. There's a large BDSM muzzle, leash, and whip hanging on a hook back there.

The sales tag is still attached to the muzzle.

I straighten the clothes back out, then move on, emboldened by the stuff I've already found. I feel a little behind when it comes to Missy, and I need to figure things out fast.

All I know is I've been on the strategy team for two weeks, and I haven't received a pay raise yet, just the ton of extra work that goes along with the promotion.

Ryan's been helping me with my presentations, but it's still obvious I don't know what I'm doing. I've been set up to fail. And Missy hasn't said a word to me since the "Congratulations" email.

She's fucking with me, so I don't feel the least bit guilty about fucking back. It's a fuck or be fucked world out there, or so my foster mom used to say when she was sober enough to dole out advice.

I feel the wall in another spot, squatting down now so I can make sure I get all areas. My hand stops on what feels like some sort of cabinet. The more I feel, the more I can tell that's exactly what it is. A cabinet with doors.

I pull the clothes to the side there and take a step back. A locked media cabinet next to the BDSM stuff seems especially promising.

Sex tapes, anyone? Yes, please.

I look around for something to pick the lock, slowly walking over to the back of the closet where the little white vanity sits with clear containers full of Q-tips, cotton balls, and… yes, bobby pins.

I pull one out and bend it into a shape that will work. Three seconds later, and voilà.

Books.

Books? That's disappointing.

It's a bookcase with three shelves. The first one is full of marketing books, mostly copies of the one Missy wrote a few years ago: *The Road to Hot: An Influencer's Journey.*

I pull one out. There are notes in the margin for the ghost writer she likes to pretend she didn't have.

In the final interview at Lagdon Marketing for my entry-level job, I met with Missy herself. A copy of her book was on her desk, and she asked me if I'd read it. Thank God I'd brought a copy. I said something like, "You know, most marketing books are irrelevant by the time the book publishes. But yours is evergreen. It's the industry standard, really. Everyone at UCLA read it. So good."

"You think? I wrote it myself. Some people think I just put my name on it."

"Those people don't know you. I actually brought that book. I was going to ask you to sign it, if it seemed appropriate, and you didn't mind."

"I don't mind at all."

On the next shelf down, there are about eight books with nothing on their spines.

I pull one of those out and open it up.

Nothing but handwritten notes look back at me. Bingo.

A journal.

I stop and listen for Jordan again, but I don't hear anything. Then, I look back through the bookshelf. The journals probably go in chronological order.

The fancier gold-leaf-type ones are right smack in the middle, probably written at the height of Missy's career, back when money was flowing in hand over fist, and she didn't have a family and a mortgage she had to spend her savings on.

The more mature-looking, plain journals are to the right of those. Floral, cheaper ones to the left, probably the ones she wrote as a kid because this narcissist has saved every word she's ever written.

I pull out three of the most recent, then sit down on the floor in Missy's closet, ready to uncover everything I can.

And get back ahead of the game.

CHAPTER 19

A part of me wants to pull out my phone and snap pictures of this so I can look through every page at home and study it. Devour it. Savor it.

But I know I can't do that.

My phone is turned off and in my car, like always. I learned a long time ago not to let your phone ping places. Never leave a trail. Even when you're just going down the street to Ralph's. Turn it off. The only pattern you should leave in life is the pattern that your phone is always off.

I also learned not to take pictures that you don't want the cops to see. Not even of a particularly deep scratch running the length of someone's Mercedes.

That stuff gets loaded to the cloud, still findable somewhere unseen, even when you're one-hundred percent sure you don't have a cloud.

I flip through the book, stopping when Jordan's name catches my eye. An entry from October.

Jordan dropped by work today with the vegan Pad Thai I like, obviously trying to make up for last night. AND he brought the boys with him. The bastard. He knows I won't make a scene when everyone's oohing and ahhing over my newborn.

But he tried to fuck another babysitter.

He told me I'm crazy, and it's all in my head. But I know my husband's looks.

And this girl is only 15.

It was our first time going out after Brady was born, and I thought I was ready to handle it. Lynette at Curvy Girls told me I didn't have to go, but I wanted to support her. She's one of my best clients, and when one of your best clients wins an award, you want as many people to know how she got there as possible.

Jordan has seemed so different lately. Distant. Depressed. I'm not sure why. I know being a stay-at-home dad isn't what he thought it was going to be. Dylan's been an absolute terror since Brady was born.

My mom says it's all normal. And I'm sure it is. But let's face it, the kid can be a pain in the ass sometimes, running around crazy when his brother is trying to sleep, tossing things into Brady's crib.

I honestly don't know how Jordan deals with it for more than a few seconds.

Which is why I thought it'd be fun to get all dressed up and get away from the kids by going to an awards ceremony together (especially after how hard that last pregnancy was for us).

I wore my Max Gregor dress, even though it was a little tight for a woman who'd just had a baby.

I felt puffy and lumpy, but Jordan swore up and down that I looked hot.

"I don't know if I'm going to be able to control myself all evening with you in that dress."

It was just what I wanted him to say. My God, it's been so long since he's said anything like that. His eyes actually lit up when he saw me come down the stairs.

Then, he barely paid attention to me at the awards ceremony. I caught him checking out every other woman, including the waitress who brought the crudités platter.

I was already fuming by the time we got in the door. And, of course, my mom was nagging me to FaceTime her because she could not believe we were going out so soon after the baby was born, so I needed to call her the second I got home.

I knew the boys would be asleep. She knew it too, but she wanted to see for herself that *"Brady was still breathing because you can't trust babysitters to put newborns on their backs, Missy. He could die."* Brady was fine. I was FaceTiming three minutes, tops.

But when I got back down to the kitchen, Jordan and the babysitter were playfully elbowing each other.

I snuck up behind them, realizing they were talking about the algebra book in front of them.

He pointed to a page and bet her that he could do any one of those problems faster than she could.

She could pick the problem. Any problem she wanted.

She asked what he was willing to bet, and he got that look that suggested it was about to get sexual.

And if he thinks I don't know that look, he's crazy. I can tell it even from the side.

He denied it when I got back from taking the girl home and confronted him. Claims it was all in my head. Innocent conversation. But a wife knows.

The way he tosses his head back whenever the girl says something. The way he puts his hand on her shoulder, softly biting his bottom lip.

I could have throttled them both. She will NEVER babysit for us again.

I curl my legs under me. A draft sneaks between the folds of my robe.

I love how jealous Missy sounds in her diary, how needy. She was right about her husband, though. I'm sure he tries to fuck everyone.

It's like she's fighting a losing battle all over the place, not just at home.

She's 30 in an industry where that's ancient. Hell, I feel old at 23.

Her position as an influencer is slipping. Out with the old, in with the new. It's why she spends so much time and money coddling her clients, personally visiting them, checking in with them all the time, trying to have the freshest and newest ideas. Being everyone's best friend.

It's got to be why she hires young people without thoroughly vetting us.

I flip back toward the beginning of the journal. I'm now invested. I want to know what happened when she was pregnant with Brady. I want to read about every insecurity she had while waddling around, being ignored by the husband she's supporting.

I stop on the word BDSM and glance over to the spot in the closet where I saw the leash.

I found some BDSM stuff last night. No shit. No kidding.

I'm huge. Much bigger than I was with Dylan. I've gained 40 pounds this time. *40 pounds!!!*

I'm pretending I love crudités platters. When I don't. I hate raw veggies. But I can't seem to lose weight no matter how little I eat.

And I still have a month left to go. I cry whenever the nurse tells me to get on the scale. The doctor says it's fine. But it's not fine.

Everything is swollen, including my nose. I look like a different person, and there are brown patches on my face that I didn't know could happen. None of this shit happened with the first kid. Not the mask of pregnancy. Not the 40 pounds. And I'm hot and sweaty all the time.

Sweaty. Like literal sweat wakes me up. The sheets are sticky and wet.

And it's like Dylan knows he'll be sharing our attention soon, so he's already being a little fucker about it. He's started biting, which is fun.

I've been looking for reasons not to come home.

Jordan suggested we get a live-in maid *and* a nanny to make our lives easier for when Brady is born, but I can't do it.

We have cleaners and babysitters already. I can't do live-ins.

I know if we start down that road, it'll end with him having an affair with one of them. Or both of them. All of them. We live in Middleton Estates. I've heard the stories about other people's husbands.

And he hasn't touched me in four months. He says this pregnancy is different on his end, too. He can "feel" the baby when we're doing it, and it's weird.

I don't even know what that means.

Then last night, after I finally got Dylan to sleep and I was cleaning up the mess in our bathroom (because there is always a mess in our bathroom, despite the house cleaner coming three times a week now), I found a leash and collar behind the door under his sweatshirt. Complete with a ball gag.

I just stared at it for a good minute, crumpled on the floor by the hamper.

I didn't touch it, and I couldn't breathe.

My uterus just kept contracting, like the worst Braxton Hicks I've ever had. One after another after another.

It honestly felt like I was going into labor five weeks early, until I noticed the sales tags were still attached to everything, and I calmed down.

He was out with his friends, but as soon as he got home — sneaking into our bedroom without turning on the light so he wouldn't wake me — I chucked the collar at him in the dark. It hit the side of his face.

"What the hell?" he said.

His eyes grew about ten times their normal size when he flicked on the light and saw what it was.

"I found it in the bathroom under your sweatshirt, Jordan. So yeah, what the hell? *What the hell?*"

"Calm down."

"Don't tell me to calm down. That's BDSM shit, and you haven't touched me in months."

He moved closer to me. "You don't think I want to touch you? I think about you all the time."

I looked away.

"It's just strange with the baby. I told you that."

"I know," I said.

He sat down on the edge of our bed and swept a strand of my hair away from my face, cupping my chin in his hand like he used to do back when we were dating. It drove me crazy then. It drives me even crazier now because my hormones are always raging.

"You weren't supposed to see this yet," he went on as he rubbed my shoulders, kneading the knots that I've been silently begging him to knead for months.

His breath tickled the side of my face. I could smell the alcohol from his night out. "I was trying to think of a way to approach you with this, honestly. I know we're going to have to wait until you're fully recovered from having Brady before we use it, but just so you know, I'd like to, when you're ready."

We cuddled the rest of the night. It was exactly what I needed.

Poor girl probably hoped they were going to use it that night. Or after she was healed from having Brady.

He's five months now, and there are still tags on the bondage stuff.

No wonder she wanted me to test things out with her husband. See if he'd have an affair.

Problem with tests is, some people fail them.

I know I need to hurry this along. Put all these journals away. Snuggle back up with Jordan. He'll be waking up soon, groggy and wondering what time it is. But I can't help myself.

I flip ahead to the last entries in the book, just to see if it was around the time I was hired.

I have to be in here somewhere. And I'm going to find those parts.

CHAPTER 20

I flip to the last page of the journal to see when it ends. I was hired at Lagdon Marketing at the beginning of this year, and this journal ends in November of last.

I go to close the book when the word Sexgiving catches my eye.

Sexgiving?

A tingle runs up my spine.

If this were the internet, that'd be clickbait. I rest my back against the media cabinet and stretch my legs out in front of me. The plush rug in here feels like I'm sitting on a cloud.

I absolutely hate people who coin new terms. It's such an influencer cop out.

That being said, I'm coining a new term this month. Sexgiving. And I plan on celebrating it every year.

Jordan and I have been fighting nonstop since

Brady was born. Over every stupid thing imaginable, like how often Dylan should brush his teeth (It should be 3x a day. Come on. Is it really that hard to get the kid to do it?) or how often I have to leave to go out of town on a moment's notice.

And now, he wants to go back to work, and I'm seriously trying to be supportive, but the thought of him around gorgeous models all day literally makes me want to throw up.

He thinks we don't have much money because we don't have much in our joint account. Plus, every time he asks for it, I think of new ways to say I'd have to liquidate something to get it. *"It's all tied up." "I can't get it until next week, honey. Sorry." "Why do you need it, anyway?"* I've learned the lingo.

He doesn't know I just don't trust him with money.

But now that he's starting to use money as an excuse to go back to work, I had to think of something.

So, I suggested he work for me again and film my catch-up segments for my channel. (People love seeing me now. My house. My kids. Holidays. Whatever.)

And I can control the amount of money I'm giving him from my business.

I've basically retired the channel, except for the catch-up segments. So doing more of those is no problem.

Which was the only reason I threw together an early Friendsgiving.

Honestly, I don't know what I was thinking. I hate Thanksgiving to begin with, because I am vegan and everyone else wants to eat animals all day.

And then Jordan started talking about live-streaming it, of all things. So I thought, "Ohmygod, I'm really going to hate this now." Because I hate cameras.

But turns out, I might do it every year.

I invited a few of my biggest clients, along with my mom and Joy. (Trust me, I made my mother swear on the Holy Bible itself that she wouldn't say anything too shitty about the tofu roast during the live stream because they're sponsors.)

The girl with the food channel did most of the cooking and even came over early to help me set up.

But before she got here, everything that could go wrong did. I couldn't wait to try the vegan gravy, so I made a batch early.

Then I dropped the entire gravy boat in the process, shattering it to pieces on the floor. Splattering the gravy onto my pajamas and smearing it into my favorite socks, because I hadn't had time to change into my outfit yet. (Thank God, or I would have ruined it.)

I was leaning over the sink, muttering cuss words to myself, dabbing at the large grayish brown spot soaking into my pajama top and reaching my belly, when Jordan came up behind me and pressed himself against my back.

I was so surprised I almost screamed.

He wrapped his hands around my middle, right over the gravy spots, and pulled me into him even tighter, whispering. "You're so hot when you're pissed about your socks."

I swung around and there he was. An extra pair of my fluffy socks in his hand. Straight from my top drawer. *Yes, one of the pairs.* I almost died. What if he would have unraveled those?

But it was so sexy and so damn irresistible.

Then, during dinner, he reached under the table and placed his hand right between my legs, squeezing my bare thigh, running a finger up the entire length of my leg.

I could hardly catch my breath.

I should have stopped him. My mother was right across from me. The boys next to her.

But they didn't seem to notice. No one did. So I casually scooted my chair in closer.

And just like I hoped, he did, too.

It's been so long since he's touched me. Never when I was pregnant. Oh no, we couldn't have that. And then, after Brady was born, he was "letting me heal."

So having him tickling my thigh drove me insane. To the point where I wanted more. He wanted more.

The camera was on us the entire time, live streaming, his fingers reaching higher and higher.

Finally, I got up and went to the kitchen to get more wine, and he followed right behind me to help. You can't see the dining room from the kitchen, but we could still hear them. My mother trying to coax Dylan into eating his mashed potatoes even though the gravy was weird. My friend Lynette telling everyone about the award she got last month, thanks to me.

I reached up into the cabinet above the sink to

grab some glasses, and he came up behind me again. This time, he never said a word, just lifted my skirt, squeezing his hands around me, pulling my legs apart.

I kept one eye on the door the entire time to make sure no one was coming in. I'm not sure I would have cared if they had, though.

I needed that more than Jordan will ever know.

I look up at the front of the closet. The door is open and darkness peeks back, but I don't hear any noises that indicate someone is awake or coming down the hall. I've memorized what Jordan's footfalls sound like on those floorboards.

I don't want to stop reading Missy's journal. I actually never want to.

This is how I'm going to stay on top of things. That narcissist obviously writes everything in her journals. I just need to make sure I put them all back in the right order, with the clothes shielding the locked bookcase, so she never knows I came in here.

But now, I need to know what was in those fluffy socks.

There's only one short entry left in the journal, and when I glance over it, I see it explains so much.

I honestly don't think Jordan will cheat on me. But he does like to flirt with other women. He likes to tease me with that, and a part of me worries it will turn into more.

I casually asked Joy to come onto him last week, right before Thanksgiving, just to see if he'd have an affair if one was handed to him on a plate. And my God, the girl acted like I'd asked her to chop her arm off and shove it up Jordan's ass.

I hear something loud fall over in the other room. Jordan's voice calls out, "What the hell?" I stand, but I don't close the book yet. I scan the rest of the entry.

> She's been in one of her "Judge Joy" moods ever since, where she thinks she's better than everyone else.
> She flat out refused to do it, which is fine, but you don't have to make me feel like shit for asking.
> Bitch has no idea who's been carrying her through life. No idea. She's about to find out.

I close the book and push it back into its spot, along with the other journals.

I take a step back and check that everything looks right, then turn off the light and close the closet back up.

Missy's painting watches me from above the bed as I rush out of the room and down the hall where I hear moaning coming from the guest room.

And not the good kind of moaning.

At least now I know why Joy sits with the rest of us, even though she's Missy's close friend.

She stood up to Missy once.

Or maybe I was just stupid to accept Missy's offer.

I probably wasn't supposed to sleep with Jordan. I was probably just supposed to *try* to sleep with him, as part of whatever this weird marital game is that they like to play with each other.

I swing the door to the guest room wide open. Jordan's on the floor next to the lamp I placed in a precarious spot, so he'd hit it if he woke up.

He's rubbing his leg, but he looks up, blinking hard from the sleeping pills wearing off, then laughs.

"Man, I am out of it. We're just lucky that didn't break. It's Missy's favorite," he says, as I pick up the lamp.

It *is* broken. He just hasn't seen it yet.

"She's had it since she was a kid." His words are a little slurred.

I hold up both pieces of the broken lamp. "We can find some glue. It's not that bad."

"It's not that bad?" He rests his head in his hands.

"Jordan, if this was really her favorite, would it be in the guest room?" I say, trying not to sound annoyed, but honestly, the man thinks about his wife way too much when we're together.

I kiss his knee, then run my finger up his bare leg, and into the warm, fleshy part of his thigh.

He leans over and kisses me back, and before I know it, nobody gives a shit about that lamp again.

And, as we hurry back into bed, there's only one thing running through my mind. I'm going to have to give him a much stronger dose of sleeping pills next time.

CHAPTER 21

BLAKE
Present Day

I freeze in the closet when I hear the knob shaking back and forth like someone is trying to get in.

Corbin didn't even knock or call my name first.

He just went straight for the door? That's strange, even for him.

I suppose it could be one of his friends. We *are* still expecting them, even though it'd be really tough for anyone to make it up at this point.

I gently scoot behind the tile and toilet paper, stepping over them, careful not to knock either of them over because I can't let whoever it is know I'm in the closet.

I stop at the frame around the closet's doorway.

"Someone's in here," I call out, like I'm in a public restroom or something.

"You okay?" It's Corbin. I breathe a sigh of relief.

But still, why did he try to *open the door* without knocking first? Thank God I locked it.

"I'm fine. I just have an upset stomach."

"Oh, okay," he says. I hear the hallway creak, then the stairs.

I stare at the door a good half minute to make sure he's not coming back before returning to the closet.

How long was he downstairs?

He must've heard all sorts of weird noises coming from up here. Me falling over, mostly.

And I have to admit, using the upstairs bathroom is suspicious in itself. There's a perfectly good bathroom downstairs… with heat. And this one is close to the attic that I declared I was deathly afraid of.

None of that is an excuse for trying to walk in on somebody in the bathroom, though.

That is just plain weird.

I try to be as quiet as I can as I make my way back through the closet, but the floor creaks.

Why do floors always creak the loudest when you don't want them to?

I picture Corbin looking up at the ceiling in the living room. He knows the layout. He'll know where I'm at.

I go down on all fours, crawling on my hands and knees, carefully placing my weight on the floor as I go. It's quieter this way, or so I tell myself.

The spot is easy to find now that I know what I'm looking for. And as I wrap my fingers back around the object, it wiggles a lot.

I flash my light on the top of it to get a better look at how to pry it out, realizing right away what it is. And why there are numbers underlined twice in that guest book.

Those numbers must be the passcode to this old iPhone.

CHAPTER 22

I tug the iPhone the rest of the way out and wipe the dust off with the edge of my sweatshirt, then run my hand along the inside wall, over the rough boards, patting down the insulation to make sure I got everything. I don't feel anything else.

Audrey must only have had time to stash her phone.

I hold it up to the light coming from my own iPhone and inspect the thing.

It's pretty beat up. The screen is cracked, probably from me yanking it out of its wedged spot behind the board. And the case is all yellowed and dingy from being back there for three years.

But it looks like it should still charge.

I leave the closet as quietly as I can, staring at the door as I step over the tile and toilet paper, still shaking my head that Corbin tried to turn the knob without knocking.

I can't imagine what he would have thought if he'd actually been able to come in here.

My backpack is just sitting on the floor with my laptop open on top of it. (Who takes a backpack and laptop into the bathroom with them, anyway?) And he would've seen worse: me rummaging through his friend's closet.

I take a second to check myself in the mirror. Dust is everywhere. The top part of my blonde hair almost looks gray. Cobwebs and dirt also coat my sweatshirt and jeans in the spots where I crawled on the floor.

I wipe everything off and even wash my face and hands, flush the toilet so it looks like a normal visit to the bathroom, then gather everything up and stuff them into my backpack, tucking the cellphone down into the very bottom, under everything else.

After checking the bathroom over to make sure I didn't forget anything, I take a deep breath and open the door, looking around in all directions to make sure Corbin isn't watching me emerge from the bathroom with my backpack slung over my shoulder.

I don't hear anything, but somehow the silence makes the hair on the back of my neck stand up again. I have no idea what room Corbin is in.

I walk toward the bedroom I've declared ours. The good one, with the queen-sized bed to the left of the stairs.

Even though there's a bedroom downstairs by the kitchen and the backdoor, it's obviously intended for children, with two twin beds in there.

Plus, I like it that the window in here faces the

driveway and the front door. It's perfect. I've already put our stuff up here.

My cellphone cord is in my backpack, and I quickly unravel it and look for a spot to charge the phone without Corbin seeing it and asking me about it.

I find an outlet behind the nightstand on the side of the room by the window and plug my charger in there. Then I tuck the backpack under the bed and run the cord to the phone while it's still in my bag.

I hear creaking on the stairs, and I jump up so quickly, I smack my knee on the nightstand.

I need to calm down. Pain shoots up my leg, but I can't let it show. I hobble-run across the room, meeting Corbin at the door as he comes in.

"You okay?" he asks. "I saw that you put our stuff up here. That was nice."

Neither one of us says the obvious. There is no reason not to take the good room at this point. His friends are not coming up.

He pulls me into him, and it's only then that I realize I'm shaking. He rubs his hands over my arms, then gently places the back of his hand on my cheek like he's checking for a fever. "You're so cold," he says.

"I'm not feeling well. I'm probably just tired," I say. I try to soften to his touch, but I know my back is stiff. I am stiff.

"I was able to get into the cellar," he says. "You'll be happy to know I found some cans of soup. I know, weird. But that's what we have. And yes, your majesty, I did check the expiration date. They're all still good."

He waits for me to respond.

"That's awesome. Great."

"And I noticed you made dinner." He chuckles at his own joke. The plates I prepared are hardly dinner. "I had some of the trail mix and…" He kisses me. "Are you sure you're okay?"

I physically will my shoulders to soften.

Sure, Corbin should have told me that his friend owns the cabin Audrey went missing from. He shouldn't have lied about going out to the car when he really walked around the backyard earlier. And he shouldn't have tried to open the door when I was in the bathroom.

But he is so thoughtful and considerate. Always has been. There is nothing to be afraid of here.

Still, I don't let myself glance back at the bed where the cellphone is charging as we walk out toward the hall because I don't want his eyes to follow mine.

"Maybe I'm just hungry," I say, looking at the stairs. "Let's eat."

CHAPTER 23

I'm not usually a fan of chicken noodle soup, but it sure hits the spot tonight. We finish the can, and everything on our plates, including some of the salad.

I didn't realize how hungry I was until I started eating. There are five soup cans left on the kitchen counter and Corbin even found some wine, too.

With the Pringles, salad, and trail mix we also have, we should be set. There's realistically enough food here for the two of us for days.

So I should feel safe.

Corbin sits next to me on the couch. We're both under the scratchy crochet blanket. He wraps his arm around my shoulders and pulls me into him.

I scoot away and take another sip of wine. "Why did you try to turn the knob while I was in the bathroom?"

"What? I knocked first."

"No, you didn't."

His face is flush from the alcohol. Our eyes meet.

"Yeah, I knocked very gently, and called your name, even. I'm surprised you didn't hear me. And honestly, I thought there was no way you were in that bathroom in the first place. You made it sound like you were never going near the attic again…"

I don't kiss his cheek like I normally would and tell him it was okay. Because it was not okay.

He pinches the bridge of his nose in frustration. "You've been carrying around a knife, for crying out loud."

We both look over at the coffee table where a knife sits next to our empty dinner dishes and his wineglass.

I'm actually carrying around several knives at this point, but he doesn't need to know that.

I set my glass next to his. "Corbin, people like to have privacy when they're using the bathroom, especially when they're having stomach issues," I say, my voice cutting.

"I know that, Blake. You're treating me like a child."

"You tried to walk in on me, and now you're the one mad?"

I hate it that he always blames the victim. And that I'm constantly explaining simple things to him. Things he should already know.

Road kill jokes aren't funny.

People don't like it when you scare them.

Don't try to barge in on someone in the bathroom.

"Sorry," he says, but I can tell. He is anything but sorry.

He squeezes my shoulders, kneading the area between my shoulder blades and my neck. And it feels amazing. I didn't realize just how tense I was.

Despite my best efforts to stay mad, I soften. He really doesn't know these things.

He lost his mom early in life, and his dad is socially awkward. And all of those things have made him the quirky, wonderful man I usually love.

I just wish he talked more about it. I know it's a sore spot. How he blew through his mom's life insurance money as soon as he got the trust at 18. Buying expensive cars. Taking trips. He only briefly talks about it, but I know he feels guilty about mismanaging the money.

He touches the tip of his forehead against mine so that our eyes are right next to each other.

"I should have knocked louder. I really am sorry."

"It's okay," I say.

He kisses the top of my head like that was exactly what he wanted me to say, then pulls away and wipes his mouth, and I wonder if my hair is still dusty from the closet.

"This is perfect," he says without mentioning the dust.

I snuggle my face into his shoulder.

And he's right. This is kind of perfect. A snowed-in getaway, the fire dwindling out beside us. No internet or phone to distract us. Nothing to do, really, except hang out.

Three hours ago, and I would've been all over this man. Now, all I want to do is ask him a bunch of questions about Audrey.

She's all I can think about. The phone charging under the bed. The code in the guest book.

"How's your stomach?" he asks. "Did you take anything for it?"

"I think all I really needed was some food."

He turns his head to the side and leans in closer, his lips already parted. His breath is sweet from the wine. I gently run my hands through the back of his hair as we kiss, realizing he's dusty too, which is understandable. Cellars are dusty places and he did just hunt us down six cans of soup. But should his hair be *this* dusty? And with little cement-like flakes. I flick one away.

"I'm going to get ready for bed," I say.

He sits up, too. "I'll finish shutting everything down and be right behind you."

I can tell he thinks we're going to continue kissing and cuddling upstairs. He's rushing around now.

I take my bowl and glass to the sink, downing the last bits of wine along the way. Then, I head up.

"Give me a minute. My stomach's still upset," I say, hopefully killing the mood.

That phone has to be charged enough for me to check it.

CHAPTER 24

AUDREY
Three Years Ago

The last bits of pink and orange streak across a dark sky, as I turn down 11th and head toward Gregory, the frontage road that runs with Main.

I don't have to go this way. I just like to change up my routine in life, but especially when I'm heading home. I don't trust anyone.

I pass the red and gold corner store I know all too well, with signs covering every window advertising for guns and jewelry.

Cash for gold. Top dollar paid. Stan's Pawn Shop.

I don't go into the parking lot this time, but I glance down at my ring finger as I drive. I only have a few weeks left on my contract, and I don't have the money yet. Stan's already extended the time "out of the goodness of his heart," which we both know wasn't really that good.

Stan saw a young, desperate woman in a tight-fitting dress.

He gave me a good loan, though, enough to put a down payment on the studio. Enough to buy some time with the new job.

"And I'll do you one better. How 'bout I don't start this contract until next month? Would you like that?" he'd said, making me touch his thick, hairy arm again. "Let's just say I got a soft spot for grandmothers."

The story hadn't been a complete lie. The diamond beetle-shaped ring really *had* belonged to my grand-mother. I'll always remember her bending down and showing it to me when I was little, running a finger over its sparkling legs and shell. "Be like the beetles in life, Aud. They can survive anything. Drop a bomb, and boom. There they are, crawling out from the dirt."

She had a million other rings and necklaces, but that was my favorite.

She just hadn't given it to me on her deathbed last year, like I told the guy at the pawnshop.

She died when I was eleven. And I stole it from my mother's jewelry box right after that.

I had to.

My mother was in one of her crazy moods, smacking her gums together, picking and scratching deep holes into her face and arms, while she and her boyfriend rifled through the little wooden box they'd placed next to their syringes.

She pulled out a handful of jewelry. *"You think he'd take that ring? What do you think that's worth? They're real diamonds, I know that for sure. My mom's son-of-a-bitch husband had money.*

And you know I won't go to the pawnshop again. What if I throw in that matching necklace?"

Fortunately, she thought her boyfriend had stolen things.

And now, I'm pawning it all off myself. The ring's the only thing I care about getting back.

A part of me knows I need to quit and get a different job. Or put more pressure on my new boyfriend for money during this "probationary period" with his wife. But Jordan keeps coming up with excuses why he can't give me any, even though I told him I wasn't making much.

"Missy's got everything tied up, babe, and she'll know. Besides, everyone's friends at Lagdon Marketing. Just talk to her and tell her you need a raise. She'll understand…"

My phone dings from my purse, and I let out a small sigh because I know it's him.

It's always him.

I don't have my real phone on right now.

He thinks we're sneaking around behind his wife's back, and I guess we kind of are. But he thinks we're doing it because we're in love.

I hit my blinker to turn onto Gregory as I pull the burner phone out of my purse, noticing for the first time that a black SUV is behind me.

And no one goes this route unless they're avoiding traffic or heading to the strip mall that we both just passed.

How long has it been back there?

That's the thing with changing up your routine in life.

Do it too many times and the change-ups become routine.

I pass a 1950s-looking truck with no doors rusting away in a field full of weeds, and up ahead of that is an old gas station with graffiti covering its boarded windows.

But that's it for miles.

If the person behind me was following me for a reason, this would be a really good spot for that reason to take place.

But I know I'm just being paranoid. There is no reason for someone to be following me. I haven't fucked with anyone in a long, long time. Or, not that they know of.

Still, I gently press my foot down on the gas pedal, and my Civic lurches into action, revving 10 miles over, then 15.

The SUV picks up speed too.

Great.

It's right behind me, with the brightest high beams I have ever seen, blaring in my rearview mirror, making it so I can't see who's in the driver's seat. Or anything.

I blink at the road in front of me. But all I see is a blurred mess of rocks and grass.

I push my foot down on the gas even farther, trying to get away. We're practically drag racing now.

And he's gaining on me. Playing with me. Revving up close, then letting up again.

I really hope a cop sees us.

There's a side street off this frontage road in about half a mile, the only one for the next four miles. I only know because I went down there when I was changing up my routine once. But I've only been down it once. Because it is worse than this road. Pot holes everywhere.

I lean forward, watching gravel and litter pass fast on the side of the road in front of me, as I try to locate the turn because if I miss it, it'll be miles of nothing.

There looks to be a small opening in the dirt ahead. *Is that it? Is that it?*

I can't tell. And I can't slow down to find out. I have to go for it.

At the last second, I take my foot off the gas and swerve to the right, the back end of my car shaking hard when I do it, and I almost spin out of control. I turn the wheel to the left to course correct, bracing myself, crashing into what has to be a large pothole in front of me.

I hit it hard, my seatbelt strangling me. But I'm safe.

The SUV didn't turn, thank God. *Will it circle back?* It was definitely a black SUV with a squarish back.

Who do I know with one of those?

I'm heading the long way now, bouncing and crunching on mostly potholes, but I don't care. My hands are shaking. And I can't catch my breath.

I kick myself for letting my guard down, for not being hyper-aware. It's my own fault.

It could be any one of the people I've fucked with in the past. It could be any one of the people I fuck with now.

But I know what everyone drives at work. I've memorized their makes, models, and license plates.

That had to be a rental car. And, the more I think about it, that also had to be Missy.

Logically, I know that if someone is *that* pissed I'm not playing her game right, then I should stop playing her game and break up with her husband.

But it's too late for that. I'm already playing, and once I start a game, I'm in it to win it.

There's nothing down this road except an RV park. I pull over to the side and shut my lights off, looking around for any sign of the SUV. I don't turn my car off, though. I don't even put it in park.

I take out the burner phone and check the text Jordan sent me.

"Is 2k enough? I can bring it to the hotel when we meet for lunch Thurs. Love you."

"Perfect!!!" I type into the text box, adding lots of heart emojis, but I erase everything before I hit send. I put the car in park and take a second to think it over.

Truth is, two thousand is not enough. Not even close. I need rent. I need my grandmother's ring back. And I need to teach my best-friend boss a very important "Don't fuck with me" lesson.

"Honestly, I need more than that, babe," I text back. *"I know you don't think she's hiding money from you, but she is. And that money is BOTH of yours. Check her sock drawer and unravel every pair. Check behind the clothes in her closet. Check between the mattresses. Those are the places girls like to hide stuff. Can't wait to see what you find. Love you! See you Thursday."*

It's a long message. I don't care. I take the car out of park and continue on my way, my smile growing to new lengths.

Let the games begin, bestie.

CHAPTER 25

I live in the modified detached garage of a house in the middle of a residential maze, which is just how I like it.

Really hard to find if you don't know it's back here, and a pain in the ass to get to.

I see my landlady's car when I pull up to the driveway. There's usually no getting past saying hi when she's home. Dawn is a talker.

And I share a porch with her, so she can see me whenever I come in. She lives in the main house, door to the left. I live in the garage, door to the right.

Today I see there's a box sitting in front of my door when I get home.

I didn't order anything, and no one knows where I live, so there should not be a box here.

I cautiously approach the porch. First, someone was following me on the way here, and now this.

My landlady opens her door when she sees me

standing over the box, which doesn't have a return address, but is addressed to me.

The smell of something savory pours out with her. I hear sizzling in the background.

"Oh hey, Dawn," I say. "I'll have the rent next week when I get paid."

"I know you will. You always do." Her living room is dark behind her. The 40-something loves to binge-watch Netflix in the dark as soon as she gets home from work. "I'm making pork tenderloins on a whim. I don't know what I was thinking. One package is probably going to make like ten. I had no idea. I'm gonna have to freeze some. You want me to bring you one when they're done?"

"Ohmygod yes. Thank you," I say, and open my door.

"Funny," she adds as I pick up the box. Her long dark hair has been thrown into a messy bun on top of her head, her thick cheeks glisten in the porch light. "That wasn't here when I got home from Costco about an hour and a half ago, and I never saw anyone delivering it."

I freeze. We don't have cameras, which was something I thought was a selling point when I moved in here four months ago.

"That *is* weird." I bring the package inside, flicking on my light.

"But I've seen a black SUV circling the neighborhood lately." She shrugs and goes inside. "I'll be over with the tenderloin when it's done. Do you like ketchup?"

I have to replay the question in my head because my mind is only thinking about the SUV. I answer way too late. "Yes, I like ketchup. Thank you."

"Do you know what that package is?" she asks.

"I think it's the special shampoo I ordered."

I close the door and set the package on the table by my kitchenette, debating the possibilities that it's a bomb, now that I know a black SUV has been "circling the neighborhood," suspicious enough for my landlady to take notice.

But then, she does notice a lot.

There's not much to my place. Dawn gives me a deal because she doesn't like hassles and needs the rent. And I pretend not to be bothered that the tile gets soaked in the back whenever it rains too much.

I pick up the package and toss it as hard as I can at the back side of the garage by my bathroom, ducking down, preparing myself for an explosion.

Nothing happens, but I really didn't think it would, so I grab a knife from the top drawer in my kitchen and walk across the room to cut the box.

As soon as I lift the flaps back, I see an envelope has been taped to a jewelry box at the bottom of the package. I open the jewelry box before the envelope because I'm a sucker for a tiny hinged box. Diamond earrings peek back.

I check the note.

Because Mondays are the worst and you are the best.

The note isn't signed, but there's only one person I joke with about Mondays, and I have been refusing to joke with him anymore, or even let him help me too much with my new job. CJ.

Is he really this desperate to get on my good side? Stalk me? Find out where I live?

I have no idea. A part of me just wants to pawn these

earrings and move on. CJ can afford it. His dad's a fancy lawyer, or he's living off some sort of life insurance settlement, or something. That guy's story always changes, but I do know he's got money.

You'd think the child of a fancy lawyer would know that stalking is a crime, though.

There's a sinking feeling in the pit of my stomach that I should never have led that guy on. I always feel sorry for the underdogs in life. And it has never served me well.

I take the note and the earrings over to my bed and pull out one of the long, plastic under-the-bed boxes. Then the one behind it.

I flip open the lid on the second one. There's an old shoebox in there, the only thing left from my first big investment in myself when I turned 18 and started my plans to get out of the halfway house. My records were sealed at that point. The possibilities were endless.

Or so I thought.

The waitressing job at the Bowl N Play required slip-resistant footwear that I didn't have the money for because I needed the footwear to make the money.

Total catch-22.

I still feel guilty about going to Walmart the evening before the interview, at the busiest time, so I could casually change out the $50 good shoes for some cheap $10 sandals, then check out with the box. I also had to steal a pair of work pants and an undershirt because the Bowl N Play required those, too.

I was going to figure out a way to pay the store back, but right after the six-week probationary period at the

Bowl N Play, they fired me because, according to them, I "wasn't a good fit."

After all I'd done to get the job.

I know the real reason. I complained when one of the drunk bowlers touched my ass.

I still have the shoebox, though. I pull it out and open it.

Under the thick wad of about twenty random folded Bible pages is a bottle of liquid laxative and the syringe I use to poke imperceptible holes into the bottom of k-cups whenever someone reminds me a little too much of the cheerleaders in middle school or the owners of the Bowl N Play.

My juicy stuff is also in here. All the things I've taken from my coworkers' desks. The receipts I know they aren't turning into payroll. And some pay stubs to use as ammunition if I ever want to pit people against each other.

Let it out of the bag who makes more than who.

I put the earrings in the bottom of the box, my eyes stopping on the newspaper articles also in there. My most treasured memorabilia.

Bowl N Play to Shut Down After Another Round of Food Poisoning; Causes Still Unknown

Anonymous Tip Exposes Drug Ring at Morrison Middle School: Honor Student and Three Cheerleaders Arrested

Couple Found Dead in Apparent Murder-Suicide; Family Suspects Foul Play

There's a knock at my front door. My tenderloin is done.

"One second," I call out and shut the lid on the shoebox, tucking it back into the under-the-bed box then sliding everything back under the bed.

Someone coughs on the other side of the door, only it's gruff and manly sounding.

It's not Dawn.

CHAPTER 26

I peek through the peephole. Just like I thought, a tall blonde man with sad eyes and hunched shoulders looks back, a bouquet of wilted white roses in his hand that he probably picked up at Ralph's on the way over.

A part of me feels sorry for him. He's just sad I'm still mad at him. And he's socially awkward, so he doesn't know how to deal with it.

He genuinely thinks that coming to a woman's house like this is okay. Sending her gifts. Following her around.

But it's not my job to teach men social cues.

I open the door a crack. "CJ, how did you know where I live?"

"I can't reveal my secrets," he says in a coy way, rocking back and forth in the dress shoes he always wears to work.

I don't think it's nearly as cute as he does. "Are you following me? Stalking me?"

His face goes red. "No. No. I would never."

He's lying.

I glance across the porch to Dawn's door. She's got her main door open, so only the metal security one separates us, and I don't hear Netflix, which means it's paused.

She's listening, probably ready to call the cops, which I really hope doesn't happen because that's another thing that has never worked out for me in life.

"Look, you can't do this, CJ." I repeat his name so my landlady will know what to say if she does have to make a phone call.

"I just wanted to tell you I'm sorry, and you won't listen to me at work." He shoves the roses at me, and I open the door a little more.

The "feeling sorry for the guy" part is winning. I take the flowers. Plus, I don't want CJ to talk about *why* I'm mad at him. Dawn works in HR. I can't imagine what she'd think if he went on and on about that.

Can you believe this guy? He told our boss how I had him move a security camera for me and how we snuck into her office together.

I am ready to scream over his voice if he goes into detail here. But for now, I keep things short and to the point. "Thank you for the flowers, but you can't come to my house anymore. I will talk to you at work."

"Promise? I can really help you with your presentations, you know?"

"I know. Thank you. Now go."

"You're no longer mad?"

"I am no longer mad."

Honestly, I could really use his help. I've been relying

on Ryan as a mentor, and Ryan isn't much better than I am.

CJ takes his time walking off the porch. He didn't mention the earrings, so I don't either. I might just pawn those and get my beetle ring back tonight.

Dawn opens the door before he's even halfway down the walk. She's carrying a plate with a pork tenderloin on a hamburger bun. "You okay?"

"Yes. He's harmless. Just a guy from work."

"He's a stalker," she says, not even waiting for him to be out of earshot. "And they all start off *harmless*. I'm gonna get a camera. That's what I'm gonna do. A couple of them. One facing the street, another for the doorbell…"

As she goes on and on about how she saw some cameras at Costco, I check the street for the black SUV that CJ has apparently rented to stalk me unnoticed. He usually drives a white Tesla.

I should've known better by now. You can't trust people just because they're weird, like you.

I don't see any black SUVs. I do see a white Tesla go by.

CHAPTER 27

AUDREY
13 years old

"You want a picture of what?" I hear Oliver say. His words are followed by girl giggles.

He's in the woods surrounding Morrison Middle. And we're not supposed to be in these woods at all, but especially not after school. Teachers check. He knows this. Plus, that stupid kid is going to miss the bus.

I drop my backpack at the edge of the woods and step in closer so I can hear them better. I tried to warn Oliver that the cheerleaders were not his friends.

But they've got his mind all twisted, so he's starting to think I'm not his friend. And he's right. I'm *not* really his friend. I just feel sorry for him because he's weird, like me. And we're both kind of new at Morrison.

Two months ago, I was the cheerleaders' target. They'd wait for me in the hall, just so they could follow me to class, chucking spitballs in my hair and asking loudly if I knew what a bra was or a bar of soap. Scooting away whenever they had to stand next to me at P.E., saying I probably had scabies.

And one time, when I didn't have anything for my period because I used to have to sneak that from Ma'am's cabinet, I balled up as much toilet paper as I could and stuffed it in the bottom of my underwear. They made fun of the lump in my shorts at P.E. It had moved all over the place. They asked if I had a dick.

I went home and told my foster mom that I needed a bra and some stuff for my period every month.

"No you don't," she'd said. "Cause the state don't give me extra money for that shit, so that means you don't need that shit."

"Yeah," I replied. "I tried to tell my teacher I didn't need it. But she asked for my guardian's number. Should I give it to her? I think they want a conference."

The only thing Ma'am hates more than buying unnecessary shit is "concerned teachers" getting in her business. She's got a lot to hide, and she thinks I don't know where she and Mr. Paul hide it.

I learned early on in life with my own mom that pretending teachers are concerned is how to get stuff. I try not to use it too often, especially with my foster mom, because Ma'am freaks out and threatens to homeschool the world, seeing how we all need Jesus, *"and they don't teach that in school."*

I never know if she means it or not.

It wasn't until Oliver came to Morrison last month

that things got a little better for me with the cheerleaders. I hear them cackling behind his back now.

He's short for eighth grade because he skipped a grade, and he's even dumber than someone who's only skipped one grade. He gets straight A's, and told me once that "he's always on the honor roll," but he's got no common sense. None. Nada. Nothing.

We eat lunch together and do our homework. He's really good at math. I'm better at history. But as soon as a cheerleader walks by, he hops up and runs over to them.

He doesn't seem to know they don't really like him.

Maybe because they started out small. They could tell he liked their attention, so they made him work for it, filming him with their thousand-dollar iPhones, asking him to make a muscle or "Show us how you dance like Beyonce again."

That poor kid really thinks the girls who shop at Abercrombie and Fitch like hanging around with the boy who blows his nose on the inside of his Target t-shirt when he thinks no one's looking.

They don't. They've got something up their sleeve.

And it looks like I'm about to find out what.

They're in a spot where I can't see them, around the bend and behind a bush. But I hear them.

"Yes, everything," Gabby says. I'd recognize her voice anywhere. "And you can't go behind the bush. Do it. Right here."

If I had a phone, I could film this. But I don't, so it's going to be their word against mine if I tell, and my words have never meant much in life.

There's a rock about the size of a baseball sitting by

my feet. I pick it up and head around the bend where I see three cheerleaders with their phones out, filming. Gabby Walker, Kelly Miller, and Jessica Hernandez.

Oliver is standing in his tightie-whities and nothing else. His thin chest almost looks concave with the way he's standing, long arms dangling helplessly by his side, shoulders hunched forward.

They are all laughing, Oliver, too. Only Oliver's laugh is thin and hollow sounding.

He's probably seeing them for who they are now.

"Take 'em off, or I'm cutting them off," Gabby says. I see she's got scissors. She raises them up to Oliver's extra-large Adam's apple. It bobs along his neck like it's trying to escape. "You wanted to hang out, Oliver."

"Leave him alone," I yell, throwing the rock in their direction. They all turn.

Oliver's face goes three shades redder.

"Run, Oliver," I yell.

"Shut up," he yells back, his voice no longer thin. The cheerleaders all smile. His face goes even redder.

Kelly steps toward me. "You heard him. He doesn't need your help. No one does, scabies. Just go on back to your trailer in the middle of nowhere."

"Maybe she wants to show us her dick, too," Gabby adds, because she's the meanest.

"That's gotta be it. She's jealous that no one wants to see it."

"No. No," I say, looking at Oliver. Our eyes meet enough for me to tell him we will not be eating lunch together anymore. "I thought I was helping, but I see you all are having a good time here. Sorry to interrupt."

I turn and walk away, kicking myself for going in the bushes in the first place, for risking missing the bus for nothing, for thinking I had one friend at Morrison when I didn't.

There are footsteps behind me, coming up fast. I hear them thumping hard along the trail. I start to run, but they have a head start on me and I can't move fast enough. Someone kicks me in the ass. Paralyzing pain shoots up my groin and into my spine as I fall to the ground.

I scramble to get up, but someone jumps on top of me.

I roll over, kicking my legs.

It's Oliver.

"Go," I yell as I try to get away from him. But he straddles me in his tightie-whities so I can't move.

He yanks my shirt up, and I struggle to pull it back down again, but I'm no match for him. Who knew this kid was so strong? My t-shirt's thin fabric tears in my hand as air shoots over my exposed belly.

"I told you she finally got a bra," he says again and again, laughing.

"Hold her down," Gabby instructs, coming at me with the scissors.

CHAPTER 28

BLAKE
Present Day

Corbin is downstairs, shuffling around the house, checking doors, turning off lights. He's moving much faster than I am.

I gently push the bedroom door so it's almost closed, but not quite, because if Corbin came up right now, he would wonder why I closed the door all the way.

The charger cord seems obvious now, the way it runs down the wall, then under the bed. I give the night stand a gentle push so it's closer to the bed to hide the cord a little better, even though I remind myself there's nothing suspicious about charging a phone.

He's not going to check what phone it is.

I pull the bedspread up, lift the phone out from its hiding spot in my backpack, and press the side button.

It takes a lot longer than I think it should, my eyes

glued to this old cracked screen, my heart thumping hard in my chest like it's trying to hurry the phone up.

But eventually the little Apple icon appears.

It's charging! It works!

There are two headphones in the side pocket of my backpack: my AirPods and my back-up corded pair. I grab the corded ones and plug them into the bottom of the old iPhone, then slip them into my ears.

I press the side button again until Siri comes on. "What's my name?" I ask.

"*That's a silly question, Audrey,*" she answers into my earbuds.

I rest my head against the back wall. Just hearing her name and knowing that she really had been here, in this cabin, three years ago, makes the hair on the back of my neck stand on end.

I hear Corbin stepping onto the stair landing, even though he's trying to be quiet.

How is he already done turning off lights and locking things up? I shove the phone and my earbuds back into my backpack.

He's hurrying because he wants to be with you. Not because he thinks you're hiding a cellphone under the bed. Relax. Act natural.

I hop up and meet him at the door before he comes in.

"I thought you'd be in the bathroom," he says, stepping into the room. "I was just going to grab my toothbrush and get ready downstairs… to give you some privacy up here."

He turns his head to the side, but he's not looking me

in the eye. He's looking at my hair, and I wonder again if he sees dust in there.

"Thanks," I say. "I'm still not feeling well."

It's not a lie. My eyes sting. My mind is racing.

"I'm sorry," he says and pulls me into him. His sweatshirt has that warm smoky smell everything gets when it's been around a fire. He brushes my hair from my eyes. "I think you're worrying yourself sick."

"You're probably right."

He smiles. "I've been in snowstorms plenty of times. If the electricity cuts out, there's a generator. All the houses around here have those. You have to when you're in the middle of nowhere."

He seems to know a lot about being in the middle of nowhere, or he's pretending to.

He has no idea I have bigger worries now.

He sits down on the bed and bounces a little like he's testing the mattress. "Ooh, this is comfy. I've never slept in the good room before."

I scoop my toiletry bag from off the floor, trying to give him the hint that he should go. But he never gets hints like that. He leans against the headboard.

"Are you going back downstairs to get ready for bed?" I ask.

He shakes his head no. "You can have the upstairs bathroom first. I've already turned off all the lights and locked everything up downstairs. So I'll just wait here until you're done. Go ahead."

I picture so many things at once. Corbin growing bored while waiting for me in the bathroom because without the internet, our phones are almost useless, so he'll look around the room. He'll find the backpack with the cord and think, "Why is she charging her phone in her backpack?"

"Come on. Let's get ready together," I say because I don't want to leave him alone in this room for even a minute, not with the guest book and iPhone I have in my backpack.

"Really? I thought you wanted your privacy."

"I think I'll be okay."

I have no idea what's going on, but I do know it's more than just my imagination being in "horror movie mode." Things aren't adding up.

Corbin had plenty of opportunities to tell me Audrey went missing from this cabin. There's no way he didn't know that.

And he sure was "checking the cellar" for a long time today.

I just don't feel like I can trust him anymore.

I look up at the attic as we head down the hall to the bathroom. I don't hear any noises coming from up there. Thank God.

Corbin scoots over at the sink so I have room. As he squeezes out some toothpaste, he talks about checking the roads tomorrow when he goes to grab the rest of the supplies from the car.

"Great idea," I say a little too eagerly. I can't wait for him to leave so I can look through the phone as much as I want without him trying to hang out.

"Then I'll teach you how to cross-country ski."

I squeeze way too much toothpaste on my toothbrush when he says that last part. It looks like a caterpillar sitting there, running down the sides of the bristles. I pop it in my mouth and act like that was a normal amount.

I do not look over at the storage closet at all as my mouth burns with too much mint flavor.

"All I want to do is sleep," I say when we make our way back to the room, in case Corbin thinks there's a chance we will be messing around tonight.

But he doesn't say anything. Or try anything. He doesn't even question why I've chosen the spot by the window when it's the opposite side I sleep on at home.

It makes me think that maybe I'm freaking out for no reason.

"I'm just glad you're feeling better," he says.

I climb into bed next to him, surprised by how good the cold sheets feel.

I almost melt into them. Corbin wraps his arm around me, and, once again, I soften to his touch.

He probably did knock on the bathroom door earlier and call out my name. I just didn't hear him because I was in the closet, trying to pry out a cellphone. There is nothing strange here.

He kisses my cheek as I close my eyes and snuggle into the smoky smell of his chest. He has no idea that I'm going to wait until he's snoring, then look through my new cellphone.

But when I open my eyes again, I'm surprised to see the room is light. Cloudy sunshine peeks through the blinds, shining on the blood red comforter.

I look over. Corbin's side of the bed is empty.

Ohmygod, how long did I sleep?

CHAPTER 29

I fling the covers off of me and hop out of bed. My head pounds out that it's not quite done sleeping, and I sit back down again, rubbing my temples, willing myself to focus. I have so much to do.

How did I sleep so long?

My mind races into paranoia. Did Corbin slip me something last night?

That would have been impossible because he ate the same soup I did. I know. I checked. From the same exact pot. Unless there was already something in the bowl he handed me…

That soup was boiling hot. The perfect disguise to mix in with something else.

The door to the bedroom opens, and I didn't even hear anyone on the stairs.

I need to get it together here.

"Hey, sleepyhead," Corbin says as he bounces into the room with an annoyingly big smile on his face.

I hate it when he calls me sleepyhead.

"What time is it?" I ask, noticing that he's already showered and dressed. His hair is only a little bit damp, too. And it's already styled with product, strategically tousled just the way he likes it so it's standing up at the top just a little.

That shower happened a while ago.

"Noon. Well, almost."

"Noon? Corbin, why did you let me sleep that long?"

He sits down on the bed next to me and runs a hand over my shoulder blades, squeezing and kneading the top part of my back.

I pull away.

"Sorry," he says. "You haven't been feeling well. And you looked like you needed it. I didn't know you had *some-place to be today.*"

His tone is cutting. There's nothing to do now but play along. And never eat anything, *anything* Corbin makes for me again.

Stop it, Blake. You've slept until noon before. Plenty of times. Later than that, even. You were just really tired last night from the drive up and trudging through the snow and digging through the storage closet. It was late when you went to bed. Corbin didn't slip you anything. Stop being paranoid.

And he doesn't know about the phone.

All I want to do is check the phone.

"Did you already get the stuff from the car? How are the roads?" I ask.

"It's really snowy out there. I think the roads are still bad, but I'll let you know. I was just about to leave for the car," he says, making my shoulders relax a little.

My eyes stop on my real phone, sitting on the night-stand, obviously not the thing attached to the phone cord, and I quickly look away.

"Don't worry. I didn't eat all the donuts," he adds. He's talking so quickly. His mind is laser focused. Mine is swirling around like a dizzying snowstorm. "And you'll be happy to know I found some coffee in the cabinet. Instant, so not great, but better than nothing. And no, I didn't check the date. I left it on the counter for you. If you check the expiration date, I don't want to know." He laughs a little.

"I'll just stick with the Diet Coke I got at the mini-mart, thanks," I say, moving my jaw around, realizing I have cotton mouth. I need water.

I look up. Corbin is making his bunched-up face again. Maybe he senses that things are changing between us. That I no longer trust him like I used to.

"You really don't look well. Are you okay?" he asks.

"Yes."

"You *can* go back to sleep, you know? Nobody's stopping you. Or judging you. We don't have anything to do today but relax and enjoy the snow… and each other." He kisses me again, and I get a whiff of his shower fresh skin. "I started the jacuzzi first thing this morning."

"How long have you been awake?" I ask, trying to keep my voice from shaking.

He shrugs and stands. "A while. I was surprised I didn't wake you with all the noises I was making, coming in and out of the room."

I stand, so he knows he should get going, realizing I'm still in my clothes from yesterday.

Was I really that tired that I didn't change out of my jeans and into my pajamas, or was I so out of it?

He stands too when I do. "There's already shampoo in the shower, and I put some towels in there, too."

His hazel eyes are desperate for me to acknowledge all he's done for us. And he has done a lot. I'm just being paranoid. I know it.

"Thanks so much, Corb, for letting me sleep in, for making the fire last night. For finding the soup…" I stand on my toes and kiss his cheek. "For everything. You are an amazing person."

He leans down and kisses my lips, gently at first, but he doesn't pull away. I can tell by the way he's wrapping his arms around my back that he expects me to kiss-him kiss him, but I pull away before it gets to be more than a quick peck.

"I'm heading out to the car while the day is at its warmest," he says. "I'll be back soon. I'm going to use the skis to make it quicker because I know you don't like to be here by yourself."

"You're going on skis?" My voice trembles this time.

"Yeah, I shouldn't be long." He leaves the room.

As soon as he heads down the stairs, I squat down by the bed and slide my backpack out from under it. Nothing looks out of place, but then I can't remember if I put the laptop on top of the guest book or vice versa.

They're all in there, though, with the phone still charging at the very bottom of it all.

But that's not the thing I've got to check first.

There's a small pocket sewn into the lining at the top of my backpack. I reach in and pull out a Ziplock bag full of brightly colored sample packs from my drug rep days. Indigestion pills. Acne cream. Anxiety meds. Pain relievers.

I pretty much brought a pharmacy counter.

But the sleeping pills are loose in a small baggy. I'm not even sure how many I brought. Maybe 15.

I wish I'd actually counted before we left. But I count them now. 10, 11, 12… There are 15. Exactly the amount I expected.

Nothing seems out of place. Not the phone or the guest book. Or my boyfriend.

I am acting jumpy for no reason, again.

I stuff all the pills back and listen for any noises downstairs.

I don't hear Corbin, which means he probably left, so there's no chance he'll walk in on me.

But I now know he will be on skis, so he'll be back soon.

Heat shoots out from the nearby vent. All I want to do is fall back to sleep. I know I need to get some food, some caffeine, maybe a shower. Definitely a shower.

But that is precious time I do not have. And those are things I can do when Corbin gets back.

I shake myself out of it and open the laptop so I can bring up the guest book messages again, and the passcode.

Then, I pull out that iPhone.

AUDREY
13 years old

I pass the green electrical box at the top of the hill where the bus always lets me off.

Snot runs onto my lip. My heart pounds so hard it feels like it's thumping in the back of my throat. And my legs sting to let me know they're done running.

But I keep going. Swinging my arms. Pumping my legs. I can see the mobile home now. I'm almost there.

What's left of my bra hangs loose around my middle, the bra strap scratching at my shoulder, rubbing it raw. I don't care.

I don't care. I don't care.

All I think is "Dear God, don't let Ma'am be home. Or that awful son of hers. Or Mr. Paul."

Sometimes nobody is.

Ma'am won't care that it was four kids on one. She

won't even let me explain. How they held me down, cut my bra, cut me in the process. My arms. My chest. My *hair*. And I had to run the almost three miles home when I missed the bus.

She will only care that she "bought this bra for me and this is how I thanked her for it."

She'll only care that I got blood on my one good t-shirt that was supposed to last me all year, and it's all torn now too.

I'm gonna sew it and my shirt. That's what I'm gonna do. I'm gonna get the blood out.

She keeps a sewing kit in her top drawer that she breaks out whenever she says I need to "fix that sock hole" or "sew that button back on."

I slow down once I get closer. I don't see Ma'am's truck. She parks right in front, and I don't see it.

My heart pounds again, but this time, in a good way. When Ma'am's gone like this, she's usually gone 'til dinner.

I hop up the lopsided porch to the door and unlock it. It takes my shaky hands three tries to get the key right.

It's my own fault for thinking Oliver was my friend when he wasn't.

He was just using me to suck up to cheerleaders.

They're not your friend, Oliver. And now, neither am I.

I run to the bathroom and look at myself in the mirror. Blood is caked around my nose. What I thought was snot was really blood. My hair's all lopsided on the side where I couldn't get away from Gabby and her scissors.

I look ugly. *Ugly. Ugly. Ugly.*

I yank the bathroom cabinet open and reach in the way back, grabbing one of the bobby pins I keep under the $200 hairbrush and the Sephora eyeshadow kit I stole from the cheerleaders.

I have to be quick. Even though I don't think Ma'am will be back for hours, I'm not sure.

She locks her room door, but I long ago figured out how to open that one. I can do it in less than five seconds now.

I should have seen it coming. The way Oliver would stop talking to me whenever the cheerleaders walked by at lunch. He'd hop up mid sentence and run over to Gabby, his fat little hand holding out a Ziplock bag of Oreos.

He never knew she was making fun of him for that. Cause he's *that* stupid. *She can afford her own Oreos, Oliver.*

He never once offered me one, though. And I was the one whose mouth would water, hoping he'd hold that bag out for me.

I jiggle the bobby pin until Ma'am's door swings open, then hustle over to her dresser, rummaging past the Bible and all the crucifixes she keeps in the bottom drawer for show. I'll grab the sewing kit in a second. I gotta check for something else first.

I was hoping when I ran up and didn't see her truck that she was out shopping because the check from the state had come in. Or Mr. Paul's disability check. Or something.

And I see now that it has. Some of the little baggies in the false part of the drawer are full of white powder. They don't think I know about those, but I do.

I grab three of the old bags, that are mostly empty except for a little residue, and open them up.

They won't notice if I take just a little piece of each of the new full bags. Not now. Not on a good day when they've got more than one new bag on top of the pile of old ones. And they're high on not only these but the fact their checks have come in for the month.

I'm careful and fast. I have to be fast.

I know everyone's locker combination at school. It's why Gabby still thinks Jessica took her $200 hairbrush. It's why Kelly thinks Jessica took her eyeshadow, too.

When I took them.

They both blame Jessica, though, because her parents are a lot like my foster ones. Only Jessica's sell and mine buy.

And that's what I'm counting on when they all get a little surprise tomorrow morning after this shit hits this fan.

CHAPTER 31

AUDREY
Three Years Ago

Like usual, the bushes back here smell like piss.

Jordan always leaves a key card for me by the back door of the hotel, like he doesn't care how it smells when he tosses it back here.

I have an hour for lunch. One hour. But I can fudge things and make it longer if I need to. No one checks or cares too much.

But I should be spending this time preparing for the meeting this afternoon. I finally have a good presentation, thanks to CJ, or I'm pretty sure I do.

I finally feel good about it, and I can't wait to see Brenda's face.

A cool wind blows through my hair as I pull the top part of the bushes back to check for the key. One of the branches snags on my good dress coat, and a wave of resentment washes over me because I do not have money to buy another coat.

And it was Jordan's idea to meet here.

The key card isn't in its usual spot, and I am not touching that random sock or digging around in piss to find it.

I look up when the backdoor opens. Someone is leaving. I run over and grab the door before it fully closes, letting myself in. Room 178 today.

I hurry down the hall toward it, clutching at my long coat, my huge cloth bag falling from my shoulder.

The Doorknob Inn is a dive and a half. I can tell the bold floral pattern under my stilettos is supposed to hide all the stains, but I can still see them there.

We only meet here because it's right across the street from Lagdon Marketing, and it doesn't have cameras. Jordan's big on that detail. So am I.

And since he was the one who suggested the place, down to the exact spot to stash the keycard, I'm guessing I'm not the first woman to come here with him. I think he loves how close it is to his wife's business. The danger of it all.

And he doesn't want to meet at his house anymore because he feels guilty about that stupid lamp.

I go to knock, but the door is ajar, so I let myself in.

The room is far from a suite. I've been here before, so I know what to expect. A bed, a dining area, some wine. I never drink enough to smell like it when I get back to work, not that it matters.

I can just see the dining table as I walk in. There's a brown paper bag sitting there that better be the money

I requested. And not another pie or a new burner phone.

The top of the bag has been curled down on itself as far as it can go, so it just shows the large lump at the bottom. Just the size of lump I was hoping for.

I won't open the bag until he officially gives it to me, even though I really, really want to run over there and grab it right now.

Did he find the hidden money in the sock drawer? What did his generous heart bring me?

I hear the bed creak as I round the corner. And I see he's found something else when he was snooping in Missy's closet.

And, like the socks, it is just what I wanted him to find. It's about time the tags came off of those.

He's naked and on all fours. His thick legs shake a little like he's not used to being in that position.

The BDSM collar is wrapped around his neck, the leash dangling across his chiseled back and down the white fleshy part of his thigh.

Our eyes meet. But I don't say anything. I sit down at the table and grab the half-empty bottle of wine, then pour myself a glass.

I take a long sip and a bite of the burger, too.

He goes to sit down, but I wag my finger. "No, no," I say. "You're not to move until I tell you to."

He doesn't say anything back, probably the ball gag.

I unbutton my dress coat. One button at a time, and let it hang loose over my body. I am naked, too, except for the heels.

He watches my every move as I place my coat on the

dining chair and sip my wine, studying the man, watching as sweat pools up along his thick, dark hairline.

But he doesn't look at me the way I want him to.

And I am waiting for those soulful eyes to beg me. To want me, like they wanted Missy in that photo that sits on her desk.

"Hmmm hmmm," he mumbles.

"No noises," I direct, as my gaze lands on the whip resting against the back wall.

We have not talked about this. We don't have safe words or gestures in place. But then, I like things better when they're not safe.

The alcohol warms the back of my throat. I pour a little more.

His entire body is shaking now.

But even among the muscle spasms and the smell of sweat along his flesh, I still don't see it. There is no love. No want. No need. No sparkle.

I make my way over to him, coiling the end of the leash around my wrist, again and again, pulling it from between his legs, smacking the end on the side of his thigh.

Then, I give it a huge yank, jerking his neck back, making him sputter. He wasn't expecting that.

Good. I have a lot more he's not expecting.

CHAPTER 32

BLAKE
Present Day

I slip the phone out of its dingy champagne colored case, and make sure there aren't any other messages tucked behind it or something.

There aren't.

I run my finger over the screen. And as soon as the phone lights up, a shiver runs up my spine, like a surge of connection to the woman who last swiped this phone. She must've been in a panic.

Desperate. Alone. Afraid.

I take another large gulp of the Diet Coke by my side and scroll down the document to find the numbers. Soda and donuts have never tasted so good, but I could only get myself to eat the donuts from the unopened package.

Logically, I know Corbin didn't do anything. He has

never done anything in the past that would lead me to believe he would give me sleeping pills last night.

But I also can't stop my mind from going there.

I punch the numbers from the guest book into the iPhone, but I'm still surprised when brightly colored apps take over the screen. There aren't as many as I thought there'd be.

She doesn't have any social media icons. Not Facebook. Or Instagram. Nothing. And there's no internet. So, none of these apps are going to work right now, anyway.

This phone is almost pointless until I get back down the hill to civilization… where I will be handing it over to the cops first thing.

Still, there must be a reason she wanted someone to find it. I go to her Notes App, looking for a message there.

There are no notes.

If she really was running or hiding from someone (and she wasn't faking her death in order to beat a murder wrap, because that thought has crossed my mind) then she may not have had much time to leave a detailed message.

I click on her photos next.

There are only five of those on this entire phone, and three of them are videos.

I don't know anyone under the age of 90 who doesn't have at least a few thousand photos on their phone. Hell, even my grandma has thousands and she needs help to get her TV to turn on.

Someone has erased the photos on this iPhone, but why?

I start at the beginning and look at things in order.

A selfie of Audrey, in the very room I'm sitting in now. Her long brown hair is disheveled, sticking out of her ponytail in crazy, frizzy spots. Her face is makeup free, her eyes watery and red.

Is this the face of a killer? A woman desperate because she messed up, and regrets it.

A video is next. I pull the charger out of the end of the phone and plug my headphones back in.

I am not ready to see whatever this is, but I know I have to do it now while Corbin is out.

I slip the earbuds in and push "play."

CHAPTER 33

Grainy footage begins, but I can't see or hear much.

In fact, there's not a lot of sound at all, just breathing and light rustling as the camera moves from side to side, trying to focus on something that appears to be the slats of the blinds in this room.

I only know it's this room because, every once in a while, I see the side yard with the driveway through the blinds. And I know that's the view here. Or it would be with less snow.

Corbin and I came in through the backdoor. But in the video, two people head up the front steps just under this window. Audrey is filming it for some reason.

There are mumbled voices in the background. I hear them now, but I can't tell what they're saying.

They are men's voices, though, and they seem to be coming from downstairs.

When the camera hits a certain angle, I see both

people at the front door have long blonde hair. No wait, one is a redhead. They are women.

I don't see faces or ages. They seem young. Under 40. I just wish I could see more.

But at least I know now there were quite a few people here when Audrey went missing. At least four. Men and women.

The breathing sounds get heavier. I know that sound must be Audrey as she films. It's followed by what sounds like the front door opening.

"Honey, I'm home," a woman's voice calls through the house as the door slams shut. It is not a friendly voice. "Bet you didn't know I was coming."

CHAPTER 34

AUDREY
Three Years Ago

I blink myself awake. My head pounds with every eye movement. It's the throbbing kind of pain that starts in your eyes and travels all the way down your neck.

I sit up, wondering where I'm at.

Think, Audrey. Think.

I am still in the hotel room where heavy, blackout curtains cover the window, like always, but I don't see any sunlight peeking in through the middle part where they don't quite meet.

And I always see that.

What time is it?

I'm going to be late for the big meeting if I don't hurry.

I bolt out of bed, but the quick motion makes my

head spin and my stomach churn. I should have eaten more of that hamburger.

I glance around for my clothes, but nothing is on the floor except my shoes. *That's right, I was only in a coat and heels.*

I find my bag with my work clothes in it, draped over one of the chairs.

I missed the meeting. I'm sure of it. I slip on my underwear and skirt.

How long had I slept?

I don't remember much past the whip.

"Jordan," I whisper-yell to the motionless mound on the bed, as I tug on my blouse and tuck it into my skirt, rushing around the room to make sure I'm not forgetting anything.

All I know is this man is going to miss picking up his kids from daycare if he doesn't wake up soon.

Not my problem, I remind myself. And I need to stop worrying about other people's problems in life and concentrate on the millions that are solely my own.

I'll have to think of an excuse why I'm this late coming back from lunch. I might lose my job, but I was already thinking that was going to happen soon. At least I have some pretty cool bullet points to add to my resume now.

Fastest entry-level employee to make it to the strategy team at Lagdon Marketing, etc. etc.

And hopefully, the brown paper bag has a decent severance package from Missy's sock drawer.

Because I at least deserve that.

I glance around the room. The alarm clock on the side of the bed says 6:15.

6:15?

It's official. I've blown it. I almost laugh out loud because I am the queen of doing that.

I know as soon as I turn on my real phone once I get out to my car that there will be a string of "Where are you?" texts from everyone at work.

Why'd you miss the meeting?

Did you have an accident?

Missy is PISSED…

I sit on the bed and smack the lump next to me. He doesn't move or wake up.

"Hey," I say, leaning down so I'm right next to his ear. "Jordan, it's 6:15. In the evening. What time do you need to pick your boys up from daycare?"

The leash peeks out from under the covers, dangling down the side of the bed like it's begging me to yank it one last time. He's facing the wall away from the door, and after slipping my heels on, I find the end and curl it around my hand.

I give it a playful tug, surprised by how easily it yanks. There's almost no give whatsoever.

The covers pull back when I do it, and I see the man's neck is purplish and mottled in spots.

Uh oh. He's going to have a lot to explain with that one.

I catch sight of the side of his face resting on the pillow, and an acid lump burns its way up my throat and onto my tongue. I gag and swallow it down again.

The leash has dug into Jordan's neck so far that I see blood around the leather strap. His face is a grayish blue and his eyes are staring off at the side wall. He hasn't blinked since I looked at him.

With a shaky hand, I somehow get myself to check for a pulse, even though I'm not sure how to do that, or if that is really necessary here. I place my fingers on his wrist. He is cold and stiff, and I can tell nothing is pulsing anywhere anymore.

"Holy shit," I mutter as I drop his arm.

All I want to do is run. As far away from this as I can. Get in my car and go. I have money now. Mexico. Arizona. Further up state. I can't stay here.

Calm down and get it together. You'll look guilty if you run. You need a plan. This isn't your first murder.

CHAPTER 35

I run to the restroom and splash water on my face to try to calm down, but my heart still races when I'm done.

The only plan I can think of is to make it as hard as possible for the police to determine I was here.

And I need to do that fast. Without panicking.

I turn the sink back on, full blast this time, and wait until I see steam pouring into the room with the water. There are three washcloths in the towel rack above the toilet. I grab one and wet it down.

I can barely touch the water at first because it's so hot, but I quickly figure out a strategy. Using just the tips of my fingers, I roll the bar soap over the cloth again and again, watching the soap bubbles rise over my hands.

Then I gently squeeze the excess water out.

I have to remember everything I touched. Everything I licked. Sucked. Straddled. Everything.

The entire length of the leash. The backboard. The

wall behind the backboard. I toss the burger, plate and wine glasses into the trash by the bed.

I'm surprised by how calm and methodical I am as I scan the room for anything else I've forgotten. The light switch. The curtain rod. Wiping the sheets for stray hairs. I go back and forth for more and more soap and hot water.

Then, when I'm done cleaning every inch of the place, I toss the old washcloth into the trash, grab a clean one, and do it all over again.

I do a better job than I did with that pie. Much. Much better. It's not even close, and that was presentable.

I get the bathroom, too, all around the toilet. The sink handles, everything.

And the man himself. Every inch of his cold, mottled flesh.

Cupping the third washcloth around my fingers, I grab the trashcan liner out from the can itself, checking to make sure both condoms are in there by the burger and fries.

I know the police will find remnants of my DNA if they look hard enough.

And they always look hard enough, damn it.

But at least I've bought myself a little time to figure things out, and thank God there aren't cameras. So no one will know when I left, or even that I arrived.

And my real phone has been off since I left work, so it can't ping at the hotel.

I actually have no idea if cellphones need to be on in order to ping places, but I sure as hell am not Googling that now.

I cannot Google anything incriminating anymore.

I tie off the trash and stuff it into my cloth bag, making sure to only touch things with the third washcloth. The crumpled paper bag looks at me from the dining table.

But the top is open now, and it's no longer fat like I remember.

I snatch it up and peek inside. It's empty.

I shove it deep into my bag, making sure my own burner phone is in there, too. The one Jordan gave me.

It is.

But the fact I didn't find *his* burner phone when I cleaned everything is what digs into my skin, like a collar.

CHAPTER 36

Dawn's got the main door open again tonight when I get home, so only the metal screen door separates us.

I quietly slip my key into the lock and turn it slowly so maybe she won't hear me.

"Hi Audrey," her voice echoes out through the new Ring doorbell. I hate the new cameras. Especially now.

I wave and open the door to my studio, but Dawn's shadow is at the security door.

She opens it when she sees me look over. Her eyes widen. "You okay?"

I realize I must look crazy. I run a hand over my hair.

"You know whatever it is, you can always talk to me about it any time. Just knock," she says, stepping onto the porch.

I back away from her.

Can I really talk to you about this, Dawn?

Wiping my DNA off a dead man's cock with a piping hot washcloth. Getting down on my hands and knees in the hotel bath-

room, trying to find every skin cell and pubic hair. Would you like to hear why I'm going to use the washing machine three times tonight?

I know it won't be long before the news crews are standing on this very porch when I'm arrested, microphones out, and Dawn will say something like, "Audrey was so quiet that night. I kind of had my suspicions."

So I can't let myself be too quiet. My excuse for missing work needs to start here. Right here. With Dawn.

"You don't look well," she adds.

"Yeah, I just had a *huge* anxiety attack." I look down at my feet like I'm embarrassed. "You know I have severe anxiety, right?"

She shakes her head no. "I had no idea. I'm so sorry."

"Oh yeah. It's bad sometimes. And I just suffered the biggest anxiety attack of my life. I couldn't even go back to work after lunch. I missed a big meeting."

I probably shouldn't have said that to my landlady.

To my surprise, she stretches her arms out and moves toward me. Her long hair is down. It swings to one side as she walks across the porch. She wants to hug me. "You poor thing."

Every part of me wants to hug her back, but I can't. What if I smell like death and a hotel room?

"I'm exhausted," I say and slide inside my dark studio. "I'm just really ashamed and worried about work..."

She points at me. "Don't be. Anxiety attacks happen, and you can't get fired for something like that. I work in HR. So I know. The Americans with Disabilities Act protects you, so don't you worry..."

I love how soft her voice is. Reassuring. I love that she

brings me tenderloins and gives me advice. And that she wanted to hug me. I will miss her.

But I don't have money for the rent. And I can't stay here.

I pinch the bridge of my nose. "Sorry, Dawn. My head is killing me, and I just want to take a shower."

It's actually not a lie. My head feels like someone has smacked it with a baseball bat, and I *have* waited to shower until I got home.

"You go lie down. Then, here's what to do next. Contact your HR department, tell them you had an anxiety attack, and apologize. Tell them you'd like to talk about options so it doesn't happen again. And let me know if you need my help. Because I know all the laws. And I have no problem bringing them up to people. None."

"Thanks Dawn," I say in my weakest voice as I flick on my light and close my door.

All I can do is walk over to my bed and sit down. It's like my body has waited until this very moment to react. To process everything.

Tears roll down my cheek and my nose stuffs up.

I was *trying*. Actually trying this time. And somehow the walls still crashed down around me.

I do not have time to cry for long. I have to stick to the plan I've created in my head. Shower three times. Wash my clothes. And not let Dawn know how much water I'm using because we are in the middle of a drought in the desert. And she will notice if I'm not careful.

I pull out both my phones from my purse.

But my landlady is right. I have to contact work with

my excuse first. I also need to text something to Jordan's burner phone that might lead police in a different direction.

If I would have been able to find his phone in the hotel room, I probably wouldn't need to be taking this extra step right now, but it's still out there somewhere, which means the police could still find it.

I realize it's got to be in his car. At the hotel. I will have to go back for it.

But first things first.

I turn on my burner phone and go to our text exchange, my eyes stopping on his last text to me.

I'll come to the hotel with the money, Audrey. But I can't do this anymore. I love my wife. This is our last time.

I drop the phone onto my bed, watching as it plops in between the folds of my comforter.

That was not Jordan.

He never used my actual name in texts. He always called me babe. And I have never heard him say he *loved* his wife. He did not *love* anyone but Jordan Lagdon.

I now know there is no reason to go back to the hotel to check for his phone. Because Missy has it.

Missy typed my name to make sure the cops would know who Jordan's burner phone was texting.

Then, she killed him.

I also know now that Missy *did* do a thorough background check on me when I was hired. She must have known about my past. Even though my records were supposed to be sealed, those things are never one-hundred percent hidden.

She talked me into having an affair with her husband, then never brought it up again.

She picked the perfect scapegoat here. The perfect player for her weird marital game. She even provided the murder weapon.

The BDSM leash, new with tags.

She wanted Jordan out of the picture, and she wanted someone to blame for it.

Adrenalin courses through my veins again.

I pull out my under-the-bed boxes, opening the one with the shoebox.

Now's the time to get rid of anything and everything incriminating. And I can't just pretend that means washing washcloths and flushing condoms. I have to start with pretty much everything in this box.

It's time to get rid of my past.

CHAPTER 37

I don't let myself think about it. Or read anything.

I knew I'd be getting rid of all of this stuff someday. And that day has come.

Simple as that.

I always thought it'd happen when I was 40, though, when maybe my husband would stumble across it or one of my kids. And I'd laugh. "Oh this? It's just a shoebox full of nothing. I barely remember what I put in there."

Then I'd look through every piece one last time before burning it symbolically when my family was at work or school. My way of saying this part of me is no longer needed. I have moved past "survival Audrey."

I am safe. And I have made it.

But nothing ever happens the way you think it will in life.

I take the box and my cloth bag to the bathroom, then shut and lock the door, even though I'm the only one in my apartment.

First, I pull out the stuff from the hotel — every dish and French fry — wiping and tossing the food into the toilet. Flushing again and again. Little by little.

I flush the condoms next.

Then, I turn on the shower, full blast hot, and put the dishes in there to wash.

Yanking down the towel from off the rack, I kick it into the crack at the bottom of the door so Dawn won't smell what's coming next.

There's already a lighter in the shoe box. I flick it on and stare at the flame for a second, watching it sway in the steam from the shower.

Am I really doing this?

I put the flame up to the Bowl N Play article before I second guess anything, watching it curl into nothing, vanishing along my fingertips.

I drop it into the toilet and light the next one about the cheerleaders and the drug charges. The Bible pages too.

1 Corinthians. Proverbs…

You can't wait to get rid of stuff until the cops come. Not when you're already three steps behind. Not when you're being set up.

Unless you killed him, Audrey.

The Bible page in my hand suddenly feels like a leather strap digging into my palm.

I release the burning page into the toilet, then turn back to the shoe box.

There's only one article left, and I saved it for last for a reason.

This one I'll read, top to bottom. One last time. I sit

on the floor on the wall opposite of the toilet, and pull it out of the box.

Couple Found Dead in Apparent Murder-Suicide; Family Suspects Foul Play.

AUDREY
Thirteen Years Old

Ma'am twists my arm as soon as the door slams shut.

Her greasy hair falls along her face, but it doesn't cover her eyes enough. I can still see them. And there's something in those wild, green eyes that tells me I've gone too far this time. She wants to kill me. I can tell.

My arm hurts and I try to pull away from her.

"I know you did it, Audreeeeey. And that's the final fucking straw. After all we've done for you. You took our stuff, didn't you?"

"No, ma'am."

"Don't lie to me."

I keep my smile in, even though I like thinking about the anonymous call. The dogs sniffing at those lockers. The handcuffs.

Oliver crying real tears. Fat drops streaming down his

cheeks as the police yank his arms behind his back and read him his Miranda Rights. His face all red and puffy.

Where's your fucking bag of Oreos now, Oliver?

"We know it was you because we think some of our *stuff* is gone, right when they found *stuff* at the middle school. Explain that, Audreeey."

She doesn't wait for me to explain. But I'm not explaining, anyway.

She twists my arm harder. "This better not get traced back to us. It better fuckin' not. You little bitch. Think you own this place. You're gonna go sit in your closet for the next week and a half. No food. Drink your own piss, I don't care. I hope you enjoyed your little prank. I'm taking you out of school. You're being homeschooled now. You hear that? You ain't going nowhere no more. Your only textbook's gonna be that Bible. Your only friend's gonna be Jesus. And you'd better pray he still loves you."

Mister Paul peeks around the corner. His eyes are bulging.

I realize he's gripping a belt in his hand as he comes at me fast. He snaps it like a whip, then hits it against the wall so hard it leaves a dent.

"Don't throw her in the closet just yet."

CHAPTER 39

BLAKE
Present Day

The second video is just as blurry as the first.

This time, the camera points down at the carpet. Brown fibers morph and fade into each other as Audrey's phone tries to focus.

Her breathing is heavy and every once in a while, I hear her mutter a curse word under her breath.

Someone knocks gently on the door.

"Audrey?" It's a man's voice. Soft and comforting.

She moves across the room to answer it. I catch sight of gray socks crossing over the carpet. The edge of the bed with its blood red comforter tucked along the sides, like a maid did it.

I doubt Audrey even slept here one night.

The camera suddenly goes dark as it films, making me think it was slipped into her pocket.

I hear the door creak open.

"I didn't do it," a woman's voice whispers.

I lean against the wall when I hear her. Because I know it's Audrey.

And I can tell so much from just those few words. She is trying to be brave, but she's afraid. Sad. Desperate.

"I believe you," the man replies.

But does he? I can't tell.

"Well, *I* don't," a woman yells from what sounds like the bottom of the stairs.

"I didn't do it!" Audrey screams. "You have to believe me," she repeats in a lower tone.

"My children lost their father! Their *father*. I lost my... Did you think... that? I trusted you," the woman yells up.

I can't hear everything she's saying because the phone is far away and in a pocket, but I hear enough. I know it must be Missy Lagdon.

She continues. "And all because he was going to break...? I found his.... So yeah, I know. Everyone knows."

I rewind that last part and play it again. I still can't hear what she's saying.

"Go," the man yells down. "You agreed to let us handle it, so let us handle it."

The stairs creak again and things get quieter, but not completely silent. It sounds like he's on the landing now, trying to talk to Missy. I hear his voice rise up every once in a while, saying things like "Nobody knows she did it."

"Oh, I know she did it." Missy yells back.

After a minute, the woman's loud voice is gone and there's only silence and heavy breathing again.

Until the stairs creak once more. Louder this time. Lots of heavy footfalls. The voices at the door are back.

"We're gonna try to get her to leave."

"She just wants to know what happened."

"Were you at the hotel?"

There are more than one male voice now.

"I don't know what happened," Audrey says. "Why is she here, anyway?"

"Joy found out we were coming up. Brenda told her, I think. This is Joy's cabin," a man replies.

"What? I wouldn't have..." Audrey begins.

"We're gonna try to get them to leave," he says.

There's something in the way one of the men's voices lilts up at the end that sounds very familiar.

More rustling follows and the video cuts out. I have no idea if Audrey meant to end the video then, or if she accidentally ended it.

There are too many people. Too many voices. I can't tell how many people are here or who is who.

But I can tell one of the men's voices is my boyfriend's voice. Because if there's one thing I know, it's Corbin.

I play it again, just to be sure.

CHAPTER 40

I glance down at my cellphone clock. I've already taken too long, and I have to hurry now.

I have no idea how long it takes someone to ski down a hill and back up in a snowstorm.

But it's probably not all day.

Plus, the last video on Audrey's phone is 45 minutes long. *45 minutes.* I'll have to sneak and watch it later because right now, I have something else I need to do.

I slip my coat and boots on, tucking Audrey's phone into my backpack again, and my own phone into my pocket.

Then I sling my backpack over my shoulder because there is no way I'm leaving it alone in this house.

And I won't be eating anything Corbin hands me, either.

I know there's probably a perfectly logical reason why my boyfriend didn't tell me he knew Audrey when I showed him that poster. Or that he was here the day she went missing.

But his voice is definitely on her iPhone. I heard it. Again and again as I replayed it.

There are a lot of things I need to figure out. But my main concern right now is keeping this phone safe until I get back down the mountain.

On my way through the living room, I place the guest book back into its original spot in the desk drawer, repeating the code for the house to myself as I approach the back door.

Is 9359 even the right one? I never punched it in. Corbin did.

I reach for the knob but stop myself, looking behind me to the pair of women's ski boots under the sign requesting you take your shoes off. I grab one and open the backdoor. Freezer-like air shoots out at me.

There's not much sunlight, even though it's afternoon. The sky is a threatening gray, but at least the snow has let up… a little.

I wedge the boot so it will keep the door open a crack, then crunch my way down the snow-filled porch steps and across the yard.

Wind pummels my face in a constant gust, bringing with it the smell of a fire again.

I try not to think about the neighbors or what could be lurking in the trees by my side. I don't look at the shadows.

I keep my back hunched forward and my head down, with my gaze fixed firmly on my wet pant legs. I'm trying to remember where the footprints from yesterday were so

I can retrace them. They're long gone from the new fallen snow.

They were more toward the trees. Maybe. No, no, they were all over.

I turn around again and again, making sure to keep one eye on the cabin. It's easy to lose your bearings in this large of a yard and in this kind of snow, especially when you have no idea where you're going.

My frozen toes tell me I should have worn the fancy ski boots and propped the door open with my knock-off rain ones.

But I don't have time to go back.

I squint against the spinning, swirling snowflakes that remind me just how vulnerable I am right now. How vulnerable Audrey must have been, too.

I scan the snowdrifts for anything out of the ordinary, until I see it. A barely noticeable wooden opening in the hill.

The root cellar.

I look in all directions, expecting Corbin to jump out at me, trying to scare me… or demanding to know where I'm going.

But nobody is here.

The snow is deeper than I thought it'd be, and it takes a concentrated effort of swinging my arms while lifting my legs to hurry this along, walking against the wind.

Corbin is on skis.

I finally reach the opening in the hill, and I can hardly believe anyone goes in this place. It's almost undetectable, and it doesn't look at all safe. Or welcoming.

But at least the locks have been busted off the door.

Corbin must have come at this with the shovel, leaving only one lock left, hanging through the looping part.

It's the only thing holding the door shut against the elements.

I unhook the lock and pull on the door slightly. It flies from my fingertips, like the wind was just waiting for someone to touch it.

The afternoon sky is a dark gray, with not much sunlight peeking through the clouds, but it looks bright compared to this cellar.

There's no electricity. No light switches or dangling light bulbs, as far as I can tell.

I can't fumble in my jacket pocket fast enough. I yank out my phone and turn the flashlight on, scanning the room before stepping in.

But the beam of light can only illuminate one small section at a time, and it takes a few seconds before my eyes have adjusted enough to see what the place truly looks like.

I close the door behind me, and it gets even darker. Something I did not know was possible.

The walls are a combination of rotting wood, stone, and dirt. Dirt is everywhere, that's for sure. I feel it. Smell it and taste it on the back of my tongue. The floor is entirely made up of the stuff.

I take three steps in, shrinking a little when the front door rattles and thumps in the wind behind me.

There aren't shelves where food would be stored. No windows. No other exits out. I would not guess there was anything edible in this place that wasn't questionable hundred-year-old jars.

Because that is probably the last time anyone actually used this root cellar.

But Corbin came back with commercially processed cans of soup and wine that hadn't even expired yet.

I tug off one of my gloves and unzip my backpack so I can grab the steak knife I have in there.

Corbin was in this cellar for a long time yesterday. Yet, I don't see any reason why.

I realize I'm actually in a hallway of sorts. There's a wooden door at the back of the cellar, so I move toward it.

I pull the door open. And as soon as it creaks on its hinge, a thick earthy smell of decomposition greets me.

But it's just a tiny dark room full of nothing.

I shine my flashlight around. More dirt. The walls are also made of the stuff back here, and the whole thing looks like it might collapse around me and bury me alive, if it weren't for the four old crooked concrete pillars holding the ceiling up in spots.

I step in farther, even though the pillars do not look sturdy enough to hold up anything.

There are shelves in this part of the cellar, but no food. Just a couple of boxes of… I scan them… zip ties and garbage bags, next to some old rags. There are also a few dusty ceramic jugs on the floor by an old barrel.

But in the beam from my flashlight, I see what I came to see.

Corbin's shovel.

It's laying in the dirt around a pile of rocks and cement that have been broken away from the one part of the wall in the back that's different from the rest because it's made of stone.

But that's not the only reason that particular wall stands out.

There's also an old rusty metal door attached to it.

What is this? A closet?

I know the house was built in the early 1900s, and that metal door had to have come from that time period. The closet could be an old hidden room for alcohol during prohibition.

Or a dungeon.

I set my backpack down by the door to the room and rush toward the metal one.

It doesn't budge when I tug on it. I didn't think it would.

I go to the hole next, kicking the shovel out of the way, so I can pull the rocks and flakes of concrete from the area around the opening there.

I'm taking too long. *Corbin's going to wonder where I'm at.*

As soon as I've brushed enough concrete away, I shove my head into the space, shining my light around what appears to be a very tiny closet within this very tiny room.

It's dark, and I don't see much, just a few mounds on the floor. Rags. And another wall about four feet from the one I just broke through. It seems like it's only more dirt… *except what is that?*

On the floor, about a foot from my face, something sparkles in the light of my phone.

A tiny diamond? A ring?

I brush the dirt away from the front of it. *Is that a beetle?*

I can't quite reach it. I sit forward more, pressing myself against the stone, extending my arm as far as I can into the hole, just as I hear the main door to the cellar fly open, smacking the wall outside.

Calm down. It's just the wind. There's no way that door is staying closed in this weather without the lock looped through it.

Or at least that's what I tell myself until I hear the unmistakable sound of shuffling steps behind me.

The room door swings open, and a bright light fills the entire space. It's blindingly bright. Like a police light.

I turn so quickly I smack my shoulder on the top of the stone wall in front of me as I blink hard against the beam coming from the doorway.

I can't see anything. Not even a shadow.

"What *in the hell* are you doing in here?"

CHAPTER 41

AUDREY
Three Years Ago

I take the long way to work the next morning so I can pass the back of the hotel's parking lot where our room was.

There aren't cop cars, yet. I have no idea what time checkout is at the Doorknob Inn, but the maid is about to need therapy.

I need therapy.

There's a mist in the air, coating my windshield, fogging things up.

I turn the dial so the wipers go faster, then faster again, but all they do is screech painfully along the glass, moaning and smearing thick desert dust into the drizzle.

I pull into the parking garage and park. I need to get it together. Keep my story straight.

As soon as the elevator dings on my floor for Lagdon

Marketing, my coworkers come at me in a rush of almost unintelligible noise, bombarding me with questions about where I was yesterday. What I was doing.

Why I didn't come back from lunch, and how come I didn't text them back.

I have to talk about my anxiety attack again and again. Being sure to keep the details vague.

"I left a message with HR. I guess we'll see how it goes."

But it's not the only thing they're talking about this morning.

Did you hear Missy's husband didn't come home last night? The police had to get involved when no one picked up their kids at daycare.

And Missy didn't even know they were enrolled in daycare.

I pretend to be interested, like everything is normal. But my stomach churns. I've forgotten to eat.

All I can do now is repeat the story about the anxiety attack. And stick to it. The police will be involved soon.

And that anxiety attack is more believable than the truth.

I've watched documentaries where the police have disregarded actual rapes and kidnappings if the victims had what they considered unbelievable stories.

The victims.

There's no way in hell some cop is going to believe I woke up next to a dead guy… who happened to just text me a message that he was about to break up with me.

Joy waves me over when I try to pass her at the coffee station. She and CJ are both there. "Missy wants to see you in her office," she says.

"Missy's here?" I cough. The words stick in my throat. "I heard..." I point back at the coffee station where people still gather. "I heard that her husband didn't come home last night."

"She's leaving soon, just finishing up a few things. She said she needed to talk to you, though," Joy adds.

I know Joy thinks I'm getting fired for not coming back from lunch yesterday. She might be right. It's the least of my worries now.

I don't stop at my desk. I go straight to Missy's office.

A part of me wants to confront her, tell her I know she killed her husband. But, I also know I can't do that because, even though we both know Jordan is dead, neither one of us *should* know Jordan is dead at this point.

Missy's door is ajar, but I still knock.

She looks up from her desk, and in that moment when our eyes meet, something passes between us.

She has won. I have lost.

She smiles and stands, straightening out her peach Chanel jacket.

"Audrey, good. Close the door. I want to talk."

I close the door and casually scan the room on my way over to her desk. There are even more cameras now. Or there are several locations where there could be additional cameras.

I'm guessing the fake plant on her wardrobe isn't hiding the only one anymore. There's also a new vase sitting at her bar, and a second smoke alarm on the ceiling that wasn't there before.

I'd have to get my camera detector out to be certain,

but it's a fair assumption this interaction is being filmed using at least three different angles.

"Have a seat," she says, motioning to the chair on the other side of her desk. "I need to make this fast. I'm sure you've heard I'm in the middle of a *family emergency*."

I nod, but I do not elaborate. "I'm so sorry."

"Dylan keeps asking where his dad is. My mother's with the boys now. I'll be leaving soon." She leans across her desk and lowers her voice. "I have to ask. Do you know where Jordan is?"

Her words take me by surprise. It's a bold move, even for her.

I glance up at the new smoke alarm. "No. I have no idea."

She bites her lip. "I see."

"I'm sure he'll turn up."

"Yes, I'm sure *he will*," she says. "It's strange he went missing at the same time you had your *anxiety attack*."

She leans back in her chair. It creaks under her weight. "I heard from HR that you didn't come back from lunch yesterday because you were having one of those. Is that right?"

"I have an anxiety disorder. It's pretty well documented, and yes, I was having a full-blown anxiety attack. I'm working on ways to make sure that doesn't happen again." It's like I'm reading from the prepared statement Dawn told me to say. "I'd like to have a meeting with HR to see what we can do."

Missy doesn't say anything. I know she wants me to mess up and link my lunch hour with her husband's disappearance, but I'm not playing along.

And that's driving her insane.

Her eye twitches a little. "You didn't have any plans to meet my husband at lunch yesterday?"

I shake my head no.

We stare at each other for a good half a minute before she finally presses her lips together and looks down at her hands. "Thank you. You can go."

I stand. There's so much I want to say, just so the cameras will pick it up. Blurt out the fact she was the one who asked me to sleep with Jordan in the first place.

She arranged our first meeting. Even brought the pie. I would never have done it if it weren't for her.

But I don't say anything. At this point, I have no idea what will be "believable" for the cops.

I open the door just in time to see a blur hurrying down the hall. It looked like CJ, but I'm not sure. *Was he listening in?*

CHAPTER 42

I spend all day looking up from my laptop, expecting to see the police walking in the door at Lagdon Marketing.

But they don't come until the end of the day, thank God. I pass them on my way to the elevator when I'm walking out with Brenda.

"What do you think they're doing here?" she says to the ceiling, turning around to follow them back over to our desk area.

The police head straight down the hall to Missy's office, even though she left hours ago.

I know now that they have found the body.

They have made the connections.

It won't be long before they will want to talk to me. And I'm not ready for that right now.

I step into the elevator and hit the garage button three times, running everything through my mind to make sure I got rid of all the incriminating stuff last night.

I flushed both condoms and most of the things in my

shoebox. I broke the burner phone to bits. Washed the plates and washcloths, and all my clothes from the hotel, including my coat that was supposed to only be dry cleaned, then tossed everything out that wasn't mine in a random dumpster behind Ralph's.

And my real phone has not pinged anywhere because it's been off.

The elevator doors open and I step into the garage. It seems especially empty today. And cold. I hear rain pattering against the roof. The whole place smells like urine mixed with damp asphalt.

And, just outside the exit, cop cars with flashing red lights line the street in the fire lane. I can see them from here. There are at least three of them.

I shiver and turn away, running my hands over my cardigan as I head across the parking lot to the spot I parked earlier.

I usually wear my thick wool dress coat on colder days, but it didn't look the same after I pulled it out of the dryer last night. It's lumpy and the lining no longer sits right under the top part.

Why did I wash it? I probably didn't need to.

I only have my backup puffer left, and it has duct tape covering a hole in one of the sleeves.

It would seem very suspicious to wear that to work at this point.

I pick up the pace.

As I get closer to my car, I see someone standing in the shadows by my driver's side door. Dark, muscular. It looks like Jordan.

Only it can't be Jordan.

Oh God, I'm seeing things. I can't fall apart now. Is it a cop?

I unlatch my purse and fumble through a wad of tissues to grab my keys, slipping them between my fingers like a weapon, as I blink at the dark figure.

It lurches forward toward me, and I gasp and back away, tripping on my own feet, falling against the car next to me.

"Are you okay?"

I see who it is now. Ryan.

I let out my breath. "Crap, dude. You scared me."

"Sorry."

"It's not you. I think I'm just having another anxiety attack, that's all. I have to go home."

He knows about my disorder now. Everyone does.

"There are police outside the garage," he says, like a warning.

"Yeah, I saw them. They went straight to Missy's office."

"Something must've happened to Jordan."

"Maybe." I shrug.

Radio chatter echoes through the garage, bouncing off the walls. We look over. Three police officers are heading to the elevator.

I freeze and stare at my key fob, but wait to hit the button until the police are heading up. The last thing I need is them looking over and noticing whose car is making a noise.

I feel like I'm already a suspect.

"I should head home," I say.

"So, yeah, we might have to postpone our trip, *obviously*. I'll keep you posted."

I realize I missed a huge part of the conversation when I was watching the police. "I'm sorry. What?"

"Bear Landing. Skiing. Hot cocoa. Remember? We were all supposed to go. We might have to postpone it because of… you know." He motions to the exit where the cops are. "Not sure what's going on."

I open my door and slide in. "Yeah, uh, let me know."

How can he think about skiing and hot cocoa at a time like this?

Because he doesn't know about the murder yet, Audrey, and neither do you.

Ryan looks across the lot when more police come into the garage. This time, they're running.

I turn on my car before he can suggest we head back up. I have to get out of here.

CHAPTER 43

BLAKE
Present Day

The beam of light shining into the cellar is the kind that's designed to blind you, disorient you, give you a headache. Like a tactical light of some sort.

I blink and turn away from it.

"C… Corbin?" I say, as I scramble to find my steak knife again.

"*Why* are you in here?" he says, his voice rising and falling in an unusual way.

But it's almost like his words are coming from someone else. His voice is deeper than usual. Angrier and muffled.

He lowers the flashlight, and I see why. He's wearing a dark ski mask that covers his entire face with only a little opening for the mouth. It's one of the vintage ones I saw hanging on the coat rack by the back door of the cabin. It makes him look straight out of a horror movie.

This whole place looks straight out of a horror movie.

I hop up from my spot by the wall.

He lifts the mask over his head. But in the harsh lighting from his industrial flashlight, his real face seems even stranger. Red and puffy. "Blake, I asked you a question."

"Stop talking to me like that. I was looking for food. I wanted to help."

"You're the one snooping around someone else's house, and you're going to get mad at me for calling you out on it? You shouldn't be in here. We have plenty of food."

"*Sorry,* I was looking for more."

He rushes across the room, straight toward me. I duck out of the way and head toward the exit.

But he doesn't seem to notice. He's not after me. His eyes are only on the shovel. He swipes it up from the spot where I kicked it, then smooths the gravel and rocks around the hole, in what must be an attempt to tidy things up.

It's not as noticeable when he's done.

"Why did you knock a hole in that wall?" I ask.

"I was looking for food, same as you."

He's lying.

"We shouldn't be in here and we need to go," he says. He bends down over my backpack, like he's about to reach for it, but I snatch it away before he gets the chance.

He looks down at my steak knife, but he doesn't say anything about it.

He points to the doorway with his shovel, and I turn to leave, but turn back around again.

"What is that? An old prohibition room for hiding and making alcohol?" I ask, casually pointing out the jugs on the floor and the cask.

He shrugs. His ski mask is still propped over his head, making his hair stick out in matted tufts around it.

He looks insane in the beam from the flashlight.

I can tell he's done talking, and I am too, honestly. The red flags have piled up here, and it's time to keep my mouth shut and my eyes open.

My brothers might have been right when they took me aside four months ago and gently explained the things they thought I didn't know about life. Incels and strange behavior. The dark corners that exist in some people's minds. And their concerns with my new boyfriend.

I blew them off. It felt like I was ten all over again, when they tried to tell me the horror movies I insisted we watch might not be healthy because the world really was full of bad people like that. Killers.

I thought they just wanted to scare me.

We both walk side by side in silence as he closes the cellar door and we trudge back over to the cabin.

I pretend to keep my focus on the snow around me. On my breath, forming little clouds whenever I exhale. But I'm really watching Corbin from the corner of my eye.

There is nowhere to run here. And nowhere to hide.

There is nothing I can do except watch my back, and try to stay alive until I make it safely back down this mountain, and who knows when that will happen.

Or if it will.

CHAPTER 44

The cabin is quiet when we get back. Neither of us says anything, even though there's so much we need to talk about.

Corbin is acting unusually strange, even for him.

I think about the man who bounced into our room not too long ago, calling me sleepyhead, with his perfectly coiffed hair, a happy lilt in his voice when he told me he would teach me how to ski when he got back.

He's a different man now as he shoves his ski mask on the hook and turns to me. I hardly recognize him. His face is pale, and his sweaty hair sticks to his forehead.

"Are you okay?" I ask.

He takes off his boots under the sign. They fall to the floor with a thud. It's like he's seen a ghost.

"I'm sorry. I shouldn't have been in the cellar," I say.

I am not sorry. I just know I need to stay on his good side until I'm safe.

"It's okay," he says. "Do you need anything?" His

voice is sweet again. If I didn't know better, I would never suspect he was angry.

"No, I'm just going to lie down. I'm not feeling well."

I don't bother to take off my boots when I walk through the kitchen. I see him behind me with a paper towel, wiping up the trail of water I'm leaving. He follows me through the living room and over to the stair landing.

He didn't apologize for talking to me in a weird tone or scaring me like I thought he would.

But an apology wouldn't work this time, anyway. I don't know how to tell him he's not coming up here with me. That he can't sleep here. That he can't be with me. Ever.

That won't go over well.

I'll have to continue with my stomach-issue excuse, so I can keep to myself until I'm back down the mountain. Then, I'll tell him things are over.

If there's one thing I learned from horror movies, it's that you have to wait to confront the killer until you have the upper hand.

You don't know he's a killer, Blake, stop.

"I'm going to get more wood from the shed," he calls up to me. I open the door to our room and go inside, locking the door behind me.

I hear him downstairs. Without other noises in the cabin, it's surprising how much you notice. He's in the living room, slamming things around, mumbling to himself.

The top of the metal bin for the firewood drops to the floor. The floor boards creak back and forth, like he's pacing. I think I hear him muttering cuss words under his breath.

The noises grow softer, like he's moving to the kitchen.

Good. He'll be leaving soon and I can assess the food situation once he's gone. See what's been tampered with and what might still be safe to bring up here.

I should grab another knife while I'm down there. A bigger one.

I don't hear the backdoor shut. But the house has gone deathly quiet.

I run to the window and peek through the blinds. I can't see the backyard or the cellar from this room, only the side of the house where the front door is located. But he doesn't come this way… if he's outside.

I freeze and listen for any more sounds.

He's got to be back in the cellar. Cleaning out that small room to get rid of the evidence.

Why did he bring me here to this cabin, knowing that he was really only coming to get rid of all traces of Audrey Randall?

You don't know that's what he's doing, Blake. Your imagination is getting the best of you again.

But a part of me knows the truth. I've seen too much now.

I rest my head against the wall by the window and try to think. I have to take a chance and go downstairs. I have to grab food and another knife. I have to prepare myself.

I also have to watch that 45-minute video on Audrey's phone.

I grab Corbin's duffle bag and open the door, setting it in the hall, right by the other room.

Then I grab my backpack and listen at the top of the stairs for any indication he's still in the house. When I don't hear anything, I head down.

The lights have all been shut off down here. Even though it's afternoon, it's still not as light as I wished it were.

Another one of my steak knives is on the coffee table, right where I thought I left it. And Corbin is nowhere to be seen.

My shoulders relax a little.

Things look normal. If he really wanted to kill me, he wouldn't have left this knife right here, out on the coffee table, for me to arm myself with.

He also would have already killed you by now. Corbin's not a killer, Blake. You're just not thinking rationally.

I move slowly through the living room, making my way to the kitchen.

The Pringles can sits on the counter next to the other four cans of chicken soup and the wine. The soup all have pull-tab tops, which is nice because I don't want to search for a can opener.

Even though every part of me would like to stuff a bottle of wine into my backpack and drink myself silly, I don't. I need to keep a clear head. I grab two of the cans of soup and the Pringles instead, just as I hear a loud thud, making me drop one of the cans and look up.

Because up is where the noise came from.

The attic again.

CHAPTER 45

AUDREY
Three Years Ago

Thank God Dawn isn't home. I don't think I could face her small talk tonight. She'd want to know how everything went with HR.

I took my time getting here, catching up on all the errands I'd put off. Grocery shopping. Closing out my loan at the pawnshop. Picking up dinner from the chicken place by Ralph's, just to make sure the dumpster had been emptied this morning. It had, just like I thought.

I look down at my diamond beetle ring that my grandmother would've given me if she'd had the chance. Her words come back to me.

You're stronger than you think you are.

I turn on my phone, and as soon as my screen lights up, texts come in from work. CJ started a group text with me and Ryan.

CJ: *You guys missed it. A shit ton of police came in. Jordan was found dead. Strangled to death in a hotel room across the street.*

Ryan: *What???? No shit????*

CJ: *Everyone is losing it!*

He sent a video. I click on it. You can't see anyone in particular, only the main office area of Lagdon Marketing. People are in their coats, like they're ready to leave. Uniformed police officers stand around the coffee station. You can only hear crying, just over radio gibberish coming from the cops. Someone says, "Poor Missy."

The texts continue under the video.

CJ: *They're questioning some of us.*

Ryan: *All that happened after we left??*

CJ: *Yeah, some news crew was outside, too.*

Ryan: *I'm just so sad for Missy.*

CJ: *Yeah, it's fucked. She's got to be devastated.*

I add in my two cents. *Just saw this. WTF!!! Poor Missy! Why are the police questioning you guys, though? Weird.*

Three dots appear on the screen to indicate someone in the thread is texting me back. The dots stop. Then they start up again.

I go to the bathroom and turn on the water to take a shower, checking everything as the steam takes over the room. The place still kind of smells like burnt paper. But hopefully the strong scent of shampoo will change that soon.

I look behind the toilet for any traces of ash or bits of the burner phone I smashed to pieces in here. There's nothing. They will find nothing. I wiped everything down, at least six times.

The shower feels good. Hot. Like it's burning away

any last bits of evidence, just the way I want it to. But it can't wash away the memory of Jordan's disfigured swollen purplish face, his eyes bugged out. His body lying there, cold and stiff.

Death has a way of sticking with you. I learned that one when I was thirteen.

I hear knocking before I'm finished.

My heart races, even though I know it's got to be Dawn with a burger or a pork tenderloin or something equally as yummy. She probably picked up takeout, the more I think about it, because she knows I've been having a rough week.

I've already eaten, but maybe I'll watch Netflix with her tonight. She's always trying to get me to do that. She's got a huge flatscreen, and pretty much every spot on her couch reclines.

I wrap myself in a towel as the knocking continues.

"Just a minute," I yell into the next room.

My phone sits on the edge of my sink and I flick it on.

CJ has finally texted back. *They were mostly asking about you. Where you lived. If I ever saw you with Jordan.*

"Police," a man's voice calls out into my apartment. The knocking turns to pounding now.

CHAPTER 46

"Give me a second. One second," I yell back, as I open the bathroom door and step into the main part of my studio. "I just got out of the shower. Let me get dressed, please. I'll be quick."

The knocking stops when I say that.

The mere fact the police aren't barging in tells me I have time. They just want to question me. They don't have enough evidence to haul me in yet.

I open my dresser drawer and pull out a sweatshirt and some joggers. I twist my hair into my towel and slip on the fluffy slippers I keep by my bed.

I glance around my studio, just to make sure I'm not overlooking anything incriminating, then open the door.

Four police officers look back, standing on the porch. Three men and one woman. All in full police gear.

That's a lot of police for this questioning. They must somehow know what's in my sealed records.

The tall one steps forward. "Are you Audrey

Randall?" he asks. He's smiling, but I don't think that's a good sign. His tightly cropped dark hair glistens in the porch light. His face is clean shaven, emphasizing a rigid jawline.

But the detail I notice the most are his eyes. Serious and saggy. They give his age away, telling me he's done this too many times before.

"Yes, I'm Audrey," I say. I don't invite them in, but I do step out onto the porch and close the door behind me.

I know Dawn will be listening to the conversation through the doorbell camera that faces the garage. *How could she not be? I would.*

"Do you work with Missy Lagdon at Lagdon Marketing?"

I nod.

One of them holds out a photo of Jordan. It's from his wedding. He's by a tree, posing in a tux with a gold cummerbund. His dark hair falls to the side of his eyes.

"Is this about Jordan Lagdon?" I ask, handing them back the photo. "My coworker texted me that he was found murdered and that you were questioning some of us from work. I don't think I'll be much help, though. I'm sorry."

"We think you will be. A big help. You can start by clearing up a few questions we have about Jordan Lagdon's murder. Did you know Mr. Lagdon personally?"

"I'm sorry. I'm very busy right now," I say.

He checks his notes. "Did you miss work yesterday afternoon? I have here that you didn't come back from lunch."

The woman officer chimes in. "Have you ever been to the Doorknob Inn?"

He glares at her. She is young like me, with eager blue eyes and thick rosy cheeks. Obviously the rookie here.

"Would you mind coming down to the police department for questioning?" he asks. "We're just trying to figure out what happened."

"I would love to comply," I say, coughing, trying to knock the tremor from my voice. I have run Google searches on this topic many times. I know it sounds like I'm reading from a prepared script, but I don't care. "Right after I consult a lawyer. Unless I'm being detained."

They look at each other again. They're hiding smiles. "That's interesting. Everyone else talked to us."

I shrug. "And I will too. But like I said, I'm very busy, and I don't talk to police without consulting my attorney first. Nothing personal. Just my policy."

"*You* have an attorney?" A chuckle escapes the rookie's lips, but she quickly composes herself again. In a different life, maybe I would have been her. The woman on the other side of this conversation, with a tight ponytail and a crisp uniform, ready to pounce if a wrong answer is given.

"Is that all?" I ask. "Or am I being detained?"

"So you're saying you're not going to talk to us without an attorney?" he asks.

"That's exactly what I'm saying."

"Have a good night," they say, turning to leave.

I quickly go inside and shut the door so Dawn can't

see my face on the camera. So she can't ask me questions through the Ring, like "What was that all about?"

I would not be able to handle that right now. But it's the least of my worries, really.

It won't be long before the police are back with a warrant, I know it.

They must have Jordan's burner phone. The way they smugly turned to each other, with knowing looks. Missy must have given it to them.

She was obviously the one who wrote the "I'm breaking up with you" text because that didn't come from Jordan.

He was very far from breaking up with me.

And I know Missy has shown them the videos she recorded in her office, too. The pie one where the camera sees Jordan enter, and a naked me tossing that Chanel jacket over the plant. You hear us, even though we're trying to be quiet, but you know we're in that room together. Doing stuff with that pie.

They probably won't be able to definitively link me to the burner phone Jordan got me because he was the one who purchased that. And it will take time for them to comb the crime scene for DNA. They have to go by the book.

They thought they'd come here and fish around for answers, but I know my rights. I do not have to hand them any piece to this puzzle.

I will need to be quick about finding a lawyer, though.

I wait until I hear the police drive away. Then I swipe my phone on and go back to the conversation with CJ and Ryan.

Soon, I'll delete everything on my phone and do a factory reset. It doesn't have anything incriminating on it, anyway, except some "Where are you" texts after I missed the meeting yesterday. But you have to make the police work for every bit of their evidence.

I bring up CJ's contact information and hit the call icon by his name.

He answers on the first ring. His voice is muffled, and he's shouting over the sounds of traffic. I can tell he's driving somewhere.

"The police were just at my door," I say.

"What? That's crazy," he replies, quicker than I thought he would, and in a tone that sounds a little rehearsed.

Did he *know* they were coming? He must have told them where I lived.

"Tell me exactly what I missed when I left work. Step by step. Don't leave out any details." I sit down on my bed and take my hair out of the towel. It falls damp along my shoulders, sending goosebumps shooting over my arms. I toss the towel onto the floor and curl into my covers, resting my head against my side wall.

"The police went straight to Missy's office. I have no idea why. It's not like she was there or anything. A couple of them started asking us questions about Jordan's murder. And that's when everyone lost it. You got the video of people screaming, right?"

"Yes. I'm so glad I left before that happened. Poor Missy."

He's excitedly telling me about everyone's reactions.

"I've never seen so many police officers."

There aren't any windows in my converted garage, and I hear noises coming from the street whenever CJ pauses. A car whooshing by. My neighbors rolling out their trashcans.

I've never felt trapped in my studio before, but I do right now. I look down at my beetle ring.

I am stronger than I think, I remind myself.

"The police took a few of us to the conference room to talk. Brenda. Joy. Me," he says. "It was like they already knew who they needed to talk to. And like I told you before, they were asking about you."

From their selection of interviews, I can tell their investigation only leads to me. I am the entire puzzle.

"They wanted to know if I ever saw you with Jordan, so I told them the truth. Only when other people were around. We all saw him. He came in a lot with their kids. Nothing out of the ordinary."

"Good. Is that all they asked about?"

There's a long pause.

"They also asked if it was true that we broke into Missy's office together, that you asked me to do it. I told them everything I knew. About that and moving the garage camera. I'm sorry…"

"Don't be. I would never ask you to lie for me," I say. "It sounds like they think I did it, though. But I didn't kill Jordan…" I hate how unsure my own voice sounds. How I'm picturing myself tugging on that leash. Harder and harder. How I woke up, and there he was…

"Were you and Jordan having an affair?"

The question takes me by surprise. I can't tell him the truth. That I only started the affair because Missy asked me to, and only kept it going to spite the woman. I can't tell him that every time I fucked Jordan, it felt like I was fucking life and everything I couldn't have.

Because I was never *that* girl. The cheerleader with the $200 hairbrush that didn't even have to ask for an Oreo. People just handed them to her. The one in the Chanel suit with the amazing career and the soulful-eyed husband.

And it felt good to be her for a little while.

"I didn't do it," I repeat, like that answers his question when we both know it doesn't. My voice rises to a high-pitched level, and I lower it again so Dawn's new cameras won't pick it up. "I swear I didn't do it. I didn't."

"Okay. Stop freaking out."

"I… I can't help it. I'm having a panic attack."

"Try to take a deep breath. I know you didn't do it." His voice has a fatherly tone to it that I didn't know he could produce, or that I needed. I can tell he wants to help me. And I want to be helped.

"Did the police tell you not to go anyplace?" he asks.

I think through my conversation with them. "No."

"Then, let's get away somewhere. Someplace where no one knows us. Make a fire. Have some wine. I can make you dinner. Would you like that? I'll stay with you the whole time until you calm down. I'd like to take care of you, Audrey. That's all I want."

I don't like how eager he is to take care of me. There's no way I'm staying anywhere alone with CJ. But, at the same time, it's exactly what I need.

"I'm just going to be honest. I think I need a lawyer. Because we both know the police think I did something I didn't do. Can you help me find a good lawyer? Your dad's a lawyer, right? I think you told me that once."

It takes him a long time to answer. I hear way too many neighborhood noises. People walking their dogs, parents gently yelling at their kids to stay on the sidewalk because streets are dangerous places. Revving engines.

He finally laughs. "Of course. I was already thinking about that. My dad's not a defense attorney, but he knows a lot of other lawyers. He'll know someone. I bet they'll do it pro bono for us. They love us."

It's exactly what I was hoping he'd say. "Ohmygod, I can't tell you what a relief that is."

"I'll talk to my dad as soon as we hang up. I'll handle everything."

I'm about to click off when he adds. "Did you like the earrings?"

The little diamonds on my ring shine in the light by my bed. "Those were from you? I had no idea."

"I thought you'd know. Our little Monday joke."

It's time to tell him the truth. He needs to know I won't be wearing those. "I should've known. I wouldn't have pawned them if I'd known."

"You *pawned* them?" He shouts so loudly, it vibrates my eardrum. "You *fucking pawned* them?"

I picture the man's neck going blotchy in spots, his eyes bulging. They were very expensive earrings. I know because the guy at the pawnshop was impressed, and he's not impressed with much.

"Just so I could get my grandmother's ring back. Oh God… I'm so sorry," I add. "Like I said, I honestly didn't know they were from you. I can get them back."

"No, no. That's the last thing you should be worrying about right now. We'll talk about all that later," he says, like he's suddenly remembering I need comforting, and he would really like to be the one to do it.

As soon as he hangs up, I hear why the parents were worried about their kids on our street. The engine revs to a new level and tires screech as someone peels by my house and down the street at a high speed.

And it occurs to me that I was so preoccupied with everything else this evening — the pawnshop, the dumpster, the police — that I forgot to check my rearview mirror to make sure no one had followed me again.

CHAPTER 47

BLAKE
Present Day

I keep my eye on the ceiling as I shove the cans into my backpack, along with a spoon.

There are definitely noises coming from the attic, but I'm not running outside again over a little shuffling and creaking.

It can't be a coincidence that Corbin is always gone when those noises happen.

It has to be him up there.

Is he trying to scare me into wanting to be with him? I have no idea, but I'm not going to ask.

I grab the chef's knife from the knife block, gripping it tightly by my side as I make my way back through the living room and up the stairs.

If I had other options, I would not be *choosing* to stay here, that's for sure.

A part of me wants to climb into the attic, just to see Corbin's face when he realizes I can hear him up there, and I know it's him. But I'd have to get a chair to reach the cord to pull down the ladder, and I'm not ready for a confrontation right now. It might be what he wants. What he gets off on.

He can explain himself to the cops, if I'm ever able to call them.

I hurry into my bedroom as quietly as I can and lock the door. Then, I rush over to the nightstand, take the lamp off, and set it on the floor.

But instead of trying to lift and slide the thing, I stare at it.

I feel foolish.

No one is running after me. Nothing is "out to get me."

But I can't *wait* until that happens to move stuff around.

I try to lift the nightstand. It's a fairly heavy, 90s piece of solid-wood furniture, which is good for a barricade, but bad for a small woman trying to create said barricade.

I manage to slide it along the carpet a little, pushing, then tugging, then pushing again, until it's braced against the door.

Corbin is going to think you've lost it, Blake, when he tries to come into this room. Because he will try to come in. This is his room, too.

That's okay if he thinks I'm crazy, I tell myself. I have new thoughts about him, too.

CHAPTER 48

I sit under the window and rest my head against the wall, so I can keep an eye on the barricade directly across from me.

The ceiling doesn't creak anymore.

Audrey's phone is sitting on my lap. I flick it on, noticing it's at 33 percent. I have no idea if that's enough to watch a 45-minute video.

But at least I don't have to hide it anymore. I'm safe to charge it as many times as I want, right there on the bed because, with the barricade I've created, I will have plenty of warning when Corbin tries to come in here.

I slip one of the earbuds into my ear and bring up the last video.

It's obviously the most important one. And as soon as I hit play, I realize right away that it was also recorded in a different location.

The camera points down at tile instead of carpet. When it moves, I see a towel. The sink. The back of the toilet where *Gulliver's Travels* sits with some magazines and the guest book on the tank there.

This must be when she created the code and hid the phone.

There's a knock on the door, and I jump, then realize the knock came from the video. Someone is knocking on the bathroom door.

"Go away," Audrey answers. Her voice is practically a scream. It bounces off the walls in a hollow, echoey way.

There's a long pause. Minutes pass where I just hear breathing. I wonder if I should fast forward. But I know I can't. I might miss something if I do. Every once in a while, Audrey calls out to go away.

The knocking continues in a rhythmic pattern. The person on the other side of that door is playing with her.

"Leave me alone."

I see Audrey's hand quietly opening a drawer. There's nothing in there, except a hairbrush and some makeup. I see the same hand open the medicine cabinet. Only aloe and makeup remover wipes.

Is she searching for a weapon?

When she closes the medicine cabinet, I get a glimpse of the same beetle ring that was in the cellar and her face in the mirror.

I pause the video.

She doesn't look anything like her missing-person poster right now. In the poster on my own phone, she's smiling, her eyes practically dancing with life.

Here, her eyes are swollen, and her face looks washed-out. Her long dark brown hair falls limply along the shoulders of her gray sweatshirt like it's giving up.

I pull my laptop out of my backpack and open up the same document where I typed the message from the guest book.

I add everything that went on in the videos so far. How two women showed up. How there was more than one man here too, and about how I definitely heard Corbin's voice in one of the videos.

That part is hard to type in there. I try to remember every detail. What Audrey looks like in the videos, the items in the drawers, the books on the back of the toilet. The ring in the cellar, and the barricade I've created.

Because if I disappear like Audrey did, maybe someone will find this document.

I try not to think that unless they find my laptop, that's an impossibility because there isn't internet here so the document isn't going to sync anywhere. I can't email it to my brothers.

A tightening ball rises up in my stomach. Desperation… to be seen, to be heard one last time. For someone to know what happened to me… just the way Audrey felt three years ago.

I hit play on the video again. Eighteen minutes have passed and it looks like it's just been knocking and her searching for a weapon.

She pulls the lid off the toilet tank. A good choice for a weapon, only it's a little too heavy for a woman to swing around easily.

She could break it into pieces on the tile in order to have something sharp. She probably knows that.

But when you're in a situation like this, where the churning in your gut says you're in serious danger, yet no one is actively trying to harm you yet, it's really hard to know when to barricade your door. When to break a window. Hide a phone.

When to start clawing for your life. Because if nothing happens, you'll look insane. And it's probably that feeling alone that stops so many of us from fighting, until it's too late to have a fighting chance.

The wall behind me shakes a little, then a lot. I pause the video and yank the earpiece out of my ear, resting my hand on the wall behind me.

It feels like the front door is opening, and Corbin has only ever used the backdoor with the keypad.

I hop up and peek between the slats of the blinds. Someone is coming into the house with an actual physical key, but I can't see who. They're hunched over, dressed all in black.

The door closes behind them.

And I'm pretty sure it wasn't Corbin.

CHAPTER 49

AUDREY
Three Years Ago

My shoebox is almost empty, now that I got rid of the syringe, the laxatives, and the articles.

The only items left are the receipts from the office that I have no problems using to make sure things go my way.

I don't want to blackmail anyone. I never do.

But if CJ tells me he can't really get a pro bono lawyer, all bets are off. There were a lot of old receipts in his desk when I first started at Lagdon Marketing. Not just the one where he and Ryan went to a strip club and paid for it with Missy's credit card. There were more.

I could also mention the stolen items in his desk.

I have a lot on him, but I will only use things if I need to because if someone tries to bring me down, I make sure I have company.

I stuff the receipts into my hoodie pocket and take

one last look around. There is nothing for me here and nothing worth missing.

But I will miss it all. Especially Dawn. I don't know what's going to happen, except that I won't be returning.

CJ offered to let me stay with him rent free if I needed to. Maybe he really is a nice guy.

The knock on my door kicks me out of my trance. It's time. I grab my puffer jacket and duffle bag and swing the door wide open.

It's early. The sun hasn't even fully risen yet, but it's a long drive up to Bear Landing, so we've got to get going.

CJ's grin takes up most of his face. I never noticed how kind his hazel eyes were before. "Don't worry," he says as he pulls me in close. "You're not going to go through this alone."

He smells like he just stepped out of the shower. His hair is still a little bit damp.

If Dawn were here, she would ask me about the cops showing up at my doorstep last night, about why on earth I'm heading out with the same guy she just warned me to be careful around.

I wave and smile to her doorbell camera like nothing is wrong, then follow CJ out to his car.

"You're going to love this cabin. It's so secluded. No internet even. The real world can't touch us there."

The tips of my hair blow in the late winter wind that's always whipping its way through our desert town.

"I'm worried about my car in the snow, though, so we're meeting at Ryan's. Ryan told me he only asked to come along because you told him to ask, and to invite all the usuals." He looks up at me when he says that last part.

Because it's the part Ryan wasn't supposed to mention. I didn't want to go away with CJ alone, and Ryan swore he wouldn't tell him how it turned into a whole get-together at the cabin. But I guess it doesn't matter much, anyway.

CJ notices my expression and puts an arm around my shoulder. "Are you okay?"

I nod.

"Good." He opens the cargo area and takes my duffle bag. "Because everything's going to work out. It always does. We'll figure out a plan for working with the police. You'll see," he says, like a man who's never had the police show up at his doorstep even once.

But I know all too well things do not always work out. Especially not when the police get involved.

CHAPTER 50

AUDREY
Thirteen Years Old

The old rickety wooden chair in Ma'am's room squeaks whenever you shift even a little, so I try not to squirm too much as I stare at the opened Bible in front of me.

She doesn't say a word. Never does.

She just sits on the good chair by the door, her greasy brown hair falling in her face as she scrolls on her phone, watching me out of the corner of her eye, her timer ticking away, making sure I don't get even one more minute than I deserve.

A loud thump comes from the front of the trailer, and she grips the armrests of her chair, digging her fingernails into the cushy fabric.

She glares at me and gets up. "You stay right here, you hear? Or I will beat the living shit out of you."

I am tied to the chair at the desk in her room, so I'm not exactly sure where she thinks I'm gonna go.

As soon as she steps into the hall, I get up. My hand is already free from the rope because Ma'am doesn't know how to tie a rope.

But I let her think she does.

Mr. Paul will be home in a couple of hours. They'll drink themselves silly as soon as he gets here. Bottle of wine. A little more coke. Or maybe that's meth. I really don't know the difference.

But that's the part I dread the most. Because sometimes when Ma'am passes out, Mr. Paul gets ideas of his own.

And they're never good ones.

With a candy bar behind his back, he opens my closet and whispers. "*Be a good girl and you'll get this Snickers. You like Snickers, right?*"

I wait five seconds then get down on all fours and feel around the carpet near the back of the desk until I find the paperclip I hid in the fibers the last time she left me alone.

It's still there. I kind of thought it would be.

I have never once heard the woman vacuum, but even if she did, she is not the type to move furniture around to do it.

Her closet's locked, and it's got to be that way for a reason. I rush over to it and jab the paperclip into the lock. But it takes me longer to get it open than it should, not sure why. My hand shakes too much and I have to hurry. She'll be back soon.

I listen for the creaks and noises she makes when she

comes down the hall. Her footsteps have a huffy "put off" feel to them. She definitely hates to have to do anything.

I finally feel the lock release and I yank the door open. The smell of musty old feet hits me in the face from the pile of shoes in the corner.

I shove the clothes to the side and feel the back wall of the closet, where people always keep their good stuff. That's where my own mother kept her jewelry box right before she beat her boyfriend with a baseball bat… over stolen jewelry that led to the cops coming and finding her meth stash.

Why do they always take kids out of a home only to put them in a foster home with almost the exact same problems?

Ma'am and Mr. Paul don't keep much back here. There's a few dusty picture frames and some belts on hooks.

The hallway creaks in an angry pattern and I turn, glancing over to the rope dangling off the back of the wooden chair. I move the clothes back, shut the closet, and hurry over to the desk, slipping my hand into the rope loop and securing it again, tossing the paperclip under the desk, trying to hide it back into the carpet fibers, using only my socked feet.

I keep my gaze glued to the Bible when Ma'am comes back, my heart still pounding hard in the oversized dress I've been wearing since none of my clothes fit anymore.

"Time to grab your shit bucket," she tells me because it's drying in the bathroom. I didn't always get to shower and clean it out. It's only been the last couple of weeks. Whenever the smell of me starts to get on her nerves too much, I empty the bucket into the toilet, hose it down outside, then take it in to dry when I shower.

It's been two months since the cheerleader incident. She called the school immediately and told them she would be homeschooling me from now on because she no longer liked the atmosphere there.

"What did you learn today?" she asks as she unties my hand.

"God helps those who help themselves," I say, like I know it's a Bible verse. She won't know either. She doesn't read the Bible herself. I shake my hand out, pretending the rope kind of hurt me, because I know she feels good about herself whenever I pretend like that.

"That's right," she says as she leads me down the hall to the bathroom, where my half-rinsed-out shit bucket still makes the room smell like a porta-potty.

I don't tell her the real thing I learned.

That she and Mr. Paul keep a gun in that closet.

CHAPTER 51

BLAKE
Present Day

There are people downstairs, and Corbin is back from the shed. They've been in the living room for a while, arguing away.

Their voices rise above my video again and I pause it, even though not much was happening in the video, anyway. It could very well be 45 minutes of breathing.

"*I know you saw us. You skied right past us…*"

"*Next weekend. Stop trying to gaslight us. I'm sure of it. You were supposed to be… next weekend… Ryan…*"

They're women's voices.

And from the small bits of information I can catch when their voices rise, they were stuck in their vehicle over night. They're sure Corbin saw them when he came on skis this afternoon.

They must have been much farther down the hill than

our car, or they would just have walked up to the cabin. It was a pain in the butt to make that little trek, but it was completely doable.

Why did Corbin ski that far, anyway? He only needed to go down the street to get a sandwich and some champagne, maybe check the roads. Was he really checking to make sure his friends weren't here? He must have spotted their car and rushed back to the cellar...

No wonder he was so sweaty and paranoid when he found me there.

I cup my hands over the earbuds and press play again.

Audrey's camera is facing up at the ceiling in the bathroom now. There's more breathing. She's pacing, asking to talk to someone... but I can't make out who.

Another angry outburst comes from the living room. Sounds like Corbin's finally gotten around to mentioning his girlfriend is here.

"What do you mean, someone's upstairs?"

"Who the fuck do you think you are?"

"Go get her. Now."

I tuck the phone into the bottom of my backpack, and walk over to the door again where the nightstand still prevents anyone from coming in.

"I was honestly confused about the date," Corbin says.

"No, you weren't."

"Babe. Babe. Can you come down here?" Corbin calls up to me. *"I'll go get her."*

I give the nightstand a huge shove so it slides out of place before Corbin can even reach the stairs, my heart beating fast in my sweatshirt with just the thought that I'm lifting the barricade here.

But I have to make an appearance downstairs.

I loop my backpack around my arm and head out.

"You and your girlfriend need to get the fuck out."

"We can't leave," Corbin says from the landing.

"Well, you're not staying here."

They hear me creaking down the stairs because I'm not trying to be quiet. They stop talking.

Corbin smiles when he looks up at me. "How are you feeling, babe?" he asks with genuine concern in his voice.

When I reach the living room, I look over at the women, but they don't even bother to smile politely. They're sitting on the long brick hearth, warming their hands and pink faces in front of the fire.

One is blonde. One is a redhead. They look older than me, but not by much, maybe ten years.

"Blake, these are my friends, Joy and… Missy," he says.

I try not to let my face drop even a little when I hear the name Missy.

"Were you stuck in the snow?" I ask.

They don't answer. *Why did they ask me to come down if they didn't really want to meet me?*

"They were here earlier," Corbin explains. "There wasn't food, so they went back into town, but the stores were all closed."

I nod. "Yeah, we were lucky to hit the Olsen Mart when we did."

"They got stuck on the way back up," he says because his friends aren't even looking in my direction, much less telling me their story. "They had to sleep in their car."

At least that explains the dishes in the sink, and why whoever it was had left in a hurry.

I try not to feel irritated that Missy is drinking my last Diet Coke and Joy is gobbling down handfuls of trail mix like it's a Costco-sized bag of it, while sipping champagne.

The champagne I once thought Corbin and I would be toasting our engagement with.

The smell of warming soup takes over my senses.

And they're making soup?

They're going to eat through all the rations on the first night.

Because they think they're kicking us out. Into a snowstorm.

I'm just glad I took the Pringles and the rest of the soup now. I don't feel the least bit guilty.

"I'd love to hang out, but…" I wrap my arms around my stomach. "I'm really not feeling well. I'm having stomach issues, sorry. I'm going to bed early."

They do not even look over.

I turn to my boyfriend. "I put your stuff in the hall so you can sleep in the other room upstairs. I don't want you to get sick. This stomach bug is the last thing any of us need."

I go into the kitchen, and Corbin follows me in there.

"It's still afternoon. You're going to sleep?"

I nod. "It's late afternoon."

"*And* you don't want to sleep with me? *For real?* You know I don't care about getting sick. I like taking care of you."

The soup simmers on the stove, and he quickly turns the heat off so it won't boil away.

He bends down and tries to catch my eye. I can tell he's thinking everything through. "Are you mad at me?

You're mad at me, huh? I'm sorry I snapped at you earlier."

I look past the fridge toward the living room, even though you can't see it from here.

He turns toward the living room, too. "Is this seriously about the rations? They were starving. *Starving. Sorry*, I let starving people eat so much, and this is Joy's house. We're lucky to be here…" He pauses, then lowers his voice even more. "I know you took two cans of soup, and that's okay."

"Glad to have your approval." My voice cuts like a steak knife. I don't want to pretend I'm not mad. This man needs to know he will *not* be sleeping in the room with me. That isn't happening anymore. His friends aren't the only ones mad at him. "I took the Pringles too."

He steps closer. "We should be fine. We're going to make it." He tries to put his hand on my arm, but I move away. He points to my backpack. "Where are you going with that?"

A part of me wants to answer him with "back to the cellar" but I don't.

It's time to be honest, though. "Corbin, I don't trust you anymore. It's why I divided the food up. It's why your stuff is in the hallway. It's why I'm carrying a knife." I hold up my backpack. "And it's why you'll be sleeping in a different room from now on."

He laughs under his breath, probably because he doesn't want his friends to hear us. But there's no chance of that. Their own voices have been angry whispers for a while. They are arguing in the living room, too.

I hear them when their voices rise.

"*Fuck them. We're not doing that.*"

Everyone is at everyone else's throats already, and we haven't even gone through our rations yet. This is about to get real ugly, real soon.

He stops smiling. "I can't believe you're serious. Look, I know you're in your horror-movie mode *or whatever*, but you're acting crazy."

"Am I? Because your friend Missy over there? You think I don't know that's Missy Lagdon?"

His eyes bulge a little and his mouth drops open. I can tell he can't believe I figured it out. He shushes me.

I lower my voice. "Why didn't you tell me Audrey Randall went missing from *this* cabin, Corbin? You must have known it."

And there it is. The part I probably should have kept to myself. I've never been good at keeping things in. This was not the time for a confrontation.

His face bunches up, but it morphs back into a smile when he catches himself. "Okay, so I messed up. I didn't want to tell you because you were already so freaked out about the snowstorm and the cabin being secluded…"

I hate it that he's prepared a lie in case this came up.

He looks back at the living room and lowers his tone. "Just don't say anything."

I don't tell him I think I saw Audrey's ring from the video in the cellar. I don't tell him my suspicions… that she didn't disappear from this cabin because she's still here, in that little room in the cellar. Or parts of her still are.

"Just know, I love you," he says. There's a finality in

his voice I wasn't expecting. And I'm not sure if he said *love* or *loved.*

His neck and ears redden in blotchy spots right in front of me. The redness spreads over his face. I can't even see his freckles anymore.

I almost want him to put that ski mask back on.

He turns and walks into the living room where his friends still argue. As soon as he's gone, I let out my breath, lean against the oven, and think things through.

I don't trust anyone tonight.

CHAPTER 52

I wake to the sound of screams.

They're blood-curdling and guttural. The kind you hear in horror movies. I was in such a deep sleep, I almost didn't hear them.

I bolt up from bed and grab my cellphone. It's 2:46, and the cries are only getting louder.

I glance over to the nightstand that barricades the door.

Do I dare go out there to see?

I shove Corbin's old pillow over so I can grab the knife that's underneath it, then slide my legs off the bed and inch my way across the brown carpet.

I press my ear against the door. Someone fumbles into the hall outside my room. Probably Corbin. He hits my wall on his way to the stairs, and I gasp.

I hear him stumbling down, sliding a little on the last few steps. He's bumping against walls. Stomping.

Five seconds later, and he's yelling, too, at someone,

with someone. I can't make out any of what they're saying because they're too far away.

My grip around the knife tightens and my back stiffens, as I listen at the door to the wailing and mumbled talking downstairs.

There's a heated exchange. Lots of loud voices.

"Blake? Blake?" It's Corbin. I can tell he's at the bottom of the stairs now, calling up to me. "Come down here. Now."

No thank you, I want to yell back. But I can't.

Because here's what they don't tell you about when real life becomes a horror movie. Everyone's supposed to help out. You're supposed to go down the stairs and see why people are screaming.

You *have* to check out the noises.

I set the knife down and push my barricade over, but I quickly pick the knife back up again.

Somehow, I get myself to unlock and open the door, peeking my head down the stairs. Corbin is waiting for me on the landing. I see him in the dark shadows down there.

"Joy's dead. *Murdered,*" he says. The smell of blood seems to come up with his words, confirming them.

My dinner of cold soup rises into the back of my throat. A warm lump now. I swallow it back down.

"I need you to keep an eye on Missy. She murdered Joy."

"*I didn't murder Joy,*" she screams from somewhere in the house behind him.

I rest my back against my door frame. "What are you talking about...?"

He has his own knife now. A butcher knife. I see the glint of it shining in the embers from the fireplace.

"There are zip ties in the cellar. I'm going to get them," he says. "We need to figure this out and call the police somehow. But we need to restrain Missy first."

I don't say anything. I'm not even processing Corbin's words.

"Blake, I need your help. I'm going to have to ski over to the neighbors. But I should tie Missy up before I go. I don't want to leave you with her unless she's tied up."

He is talking slowly, enunciating every syllable, so maybe I'll snap out of it and understand. He waves his hand in my direction. "Do you hear what I'm saying? Missy murdered Joy, and I need you to watch her. Just keep your knife trained on her for a short while, while I get the zip ties, and then again while I ski over to a phone. I need your help."

I gulp and motion with my knife. "Back away and walk toward the backdoor first," I say, as I try to think through what he's telling me.

"You *still* don't trust me," he says, but it's not a question. He leaves through the house.

I hear Missy mumbling incoherently somewhere downstairs, but I can't make out a word she's saying.

I grab my backpack, then slowly head down. But I stop at the landing and look around the dark living room. "Corbin, I don't see you. Where are you?"

He calls out from the back of the house. "I'm putting my coat on. I'm at the backdoor. I'm not leaving for the cellar until I see you with Missy, though. *Because I don't trust her.*"

It's a long walk through the dim living room. Each step brings the thick smell of death a little closer. I pass through the kitchen and stop in my tracks.

There are blood-covered legs in the hall. I see them there. Purple and mottled. Blood has pooled up everywhere. There are bloody footprints in the kitchen.

"I don't want to deal with this," I mumble.

"You're okay," he says in a surprisingly calm voice. "Just don't let her out of your sight. Keep your knife ready. I'm going outside now."

I hear the backdoor opening.

I continue making my way to the scene where Missy is curled in the fetal position under the coat rack in the middle of the hall, rocking back and forth, with her friend Joy lying stiff by her side in the doorway of the downstairs bedroom.

A knife sticks out of her neck.

Missy is covered in blood. Joy is too. There's so much blood. Too much blood.

"I know. It's bad," Corbin says from the doorway. "Maybe she'll tell you why she did it. Ask her. A lot happened after you went to bed. I'll tell you about it later. But she… uh, has Audrey Randall's ring in her pocket. I saw her put it there."

He steps onto the porch. I feel the knife going limp in my hand, so I grip it tighter. Pain shoots over my palm when I do it. I realize I've cut myself somewhere along the way.

"Just keep your knife on her. It's going to take a while to get to the cellar and back in this snow."

The door closes.

Missy sits up when he leaves and makes eye contact with me. "I found Joy like that. I dragged her out of bed to see if I could do CPR. I don't even know CPR..." Missy's voice rises and falls unnaturally when she talks.

She motions with her head toward the backdoor. "If we both want to make it out of here alive, we need to work together. And fast. I didn't kill anybody."

I unzip my backpack as she continues talking. "I don't believe you."

"I know you don't know me. But I *didn't* do it. I *didn't* do anything. You shouldn't believe your boyfriend. Joy was my best friend. Why would I kill her?"

I bring out Audrey's phone. "I don't believe you, but not because of my boyfriend. I don't because of this."

She blinks at the phone. "What is that?" Her eyes focus on it. "Where did you get that?"

"I found it here in the cabin." I shake it. "And it explains *why* you did it. You found out who really killed your husband three years ago, and you freaked out... because you murdered the wrong woman over it back then. Your *best friend* lied to you. So you murdered the real killer now."

She rests her head against the back wall and closes her eyes. Caked on blood is in her hair and along the side of her cheek. "I don't know what you're talking about."

With shaky hands, I bring up the last video and push play. It's already cued to the right spot. Because I watched it over and over again.

CHAPTER 53

AUDREY
Three Years Ago

"I can wait as long as you can," Joy says from the other side of the door.

I don't say a word. I have the toilet tank lid gripped firmly in my hands. And I'm not even sure why. The edges are rough and the whole thing is hard to hold. Plus, carrying a weapon seems silly right now.

Do I really expect her to come crashing through that door?

"I told Missy not to hire you," she continues. "But she didn't listen. So I started checking things on my own. Bullet points on your resume. One by one. I don't think anything was the truth, was it? Red flags were every-where. *Everywhere.* I told Missy we should do a full back-ground check on you. *Easy to do* with Missy's connections. You'll *never* believe what we found when we got that report back."

The bathroom is very small. There isn't a window in here, just a skylight at the top to bring in light. There's no way for me to escape.

Missy *did* set me up to take the fall on her husband. She *did* know about my sealed record, just like I thought.

Joy is still talking. "Yes. We know *everything*. Jordan wasn't even your first murder, was he? Did you think we wouldn't find out about your foster parents? You should have seen Missy's face when I told her. It was priceless. I wasn't shocked at all."

I back up so I'm braced against the closet door. The tank lid starts to get heavy, but I don't even lower it a little.

She can easily get in here. That lock is basic and just for show. But maybe normal people don't know about locks like I do.

There are people downstairs, Audrey. She's not going to try anything with them around.

Her heavy breathing almost echoes through the bathroom. She must have her face pressed right against the crack between the door and the frame. "Tell me… how did it feel? Choking Jordan to death after all Missy did for you? Tugging harder and harder… just because he was going to break up with you. And your sugar daddy days were over. Missy found his burner phone. She gave it to the police. Everybody knows."

It feels like she's putting on a show for the people downstairs. Or maybe she's recording me, trying to get me to confess to something I didn't do, and I'm done doing that…

But she does seem to be overly mad about things. Overly invested.

It all hits me. "*You* did it."

"Nice try."

My voice grows louder. I am taking over the show for the audience downstairs. "Oh no, I'm not *trying*, Joy. I know. Missy asked me to sleep with Jordan, and that's the only reason I slept with him. Just like she asked *you* to try to sleep with Jordan right before Thanksgiving last year. But *you* said no. *You said no.* Because you didn't know what to say when your best friend asked you to do something… *that you were already doing.*"

I don't give her a chance to respond. I keep talking. "You probably met at the Doorknob Inn, huh? I knew I wasn't the first girl he took there. That's how you knew he always left a key behind the bush by the backdoor, which explains why there wasn't one the day he died…"

"You're admitting you were at the hotel?" Her voice gets louder. She *is* recording this.

She doesn't know that I'm recording it too.

She wants me to be rattled and mess up.

But that's not happening. "There wasn't a key because you took it. You drugged us, maybe intercepted the wine and lunch coming to the room. I don't know. We can ask the waitstaff to see."

There's a slight laugh. I'm hitting on something. A lot of somethings.

More comes to me. "Ohmygod, *you* snuck in and choked Jordan to death with the BDSM leash and collar that *you* bought for him. It all makes sense now. Did Missy tell you it went missing from her closet?"

"What are you talking about? You're desperate."

"Am I? That must have been your breaking point. Knowing how he was using that with me."

I rest the tank lid on the wall by the closet and stretch my fingers out. They hurt from the way they were curled around the edge of that porcelain for long long.

Then, I reach into my sweatshirt pocket and pull out the handful of receipts that I kept from my shoebox. I sift through them all until I find the one I'm thinking of and show it to the camera, taking a picture of it while the video still records. My hand is shaky, and the camera can't quite focus. I set the receipt down on the edge of the sink next to the guest book, and make sure I get a good steady shot of this one.

As soon as I do, I slip the paper under the door, and prepare for Joy to freak out. "Your name's on that, Joy. I bet they can trace what it was for, too. I'm guessing from the price, the date, and the store that it's a collection of BDSM items. Paid for on the company credit card because Missy never checks. Did you get off on using that card? Did you get off on meeting Jordan at the hotel across the street from his wife's work? *Your best friend.*"

She finally grabs the receipt from under the door. I hear it ripping to pieces. "Bitch!"

I'm pretty sure she's no longer recording this, but I'm still hoping that everyone else can hear me.

"I snuck into your desk at work," I yell, my face close to the door so the people downstairs can't help but hear, too. "Pretty *easy to do* with my background that you found all about with *your connections.* A bunch of receipts were in your locked bottom drawer, under the false bottom. This is just one of them. You always had the most questionable ones out of everyone in the office. Funny, I thought that grainy polaroid that's also in there was of Ryan. But it was Jordan's side of his face, sleeping. Do you always take pictures of men sleeping? Or just the extremely good-looking ones that you were in love with? Did he drop you when he started seeing me?"

Joy kicks the door hard. Again and again. She stops kicking and laughs. It's almost maniacal sounding. I know I'm right. Everything I've said is right.

She is the desperate one now. Things go quiet.

Too quiet.

I realize I don't hear anyone else in the house like I thought I would. No quiet shuffling downstairs. No muffled conversations. No one running up the stairs to help, like you would expect them to do, after hearing me yelling about who the real killer was.

Did they all leave? My God, what if it's just us here?

I need to hide my phone. And fast. I can always come back for it. But it has everything on it. My heart thumps hard in my chest as I scan the room for options.

The closet is my best bet. I quietly open the door and duck in there to look around.

There are unfinished boards everywhere and insulation. I bet I could wedge this thing behind one of them.

Joy's still talking to me, or maybe she's talking to herself. Rambling on like a crazy person.

"Missy's gone. She left. So I don't know who you thought you were yelling all that out to. She went back down the mountain with the others because she didn't *like all this tension*. So they're gone. There's no one here. But us."

After finding a good spot, I come out of the closet and eye the guest book resting on the sink with the rest of the bathroom reading material, a pencil dangling down from it on a string.

I open to a random page and start underlining letters. *AUDREYRAN…*

If worst comes to worst, and I highly doubt it will because I can take this woman on, maybe someone will find this book and my phone.

Because Joy doesn't know I'm making this video, and if I suddenly disappear, this will be all I have left.

"I'm sure we can find you a lawyer, Joy," I call out as I look up from the guest book, trying to buy myself more time. I have to hurry. "It'll go easier if you confess. CJ's dad's a lawyer. Maybe. He knows lawyers…"

She stops laughing. "You're serious, aren't you? You really think you're going to make it out of here. Missy and I only came here for one reason. And she was the one who came up with it. She even handed me this gun, took everyone back down the mountain…"

I gulp.

"And told me to '*Kill the bitch,*'" she adds. "Do not let her leave."

The words already hit me like a bullet.

"She couldn't do it herself. I told her I could, no problem."

I have a feeling Joy won't shoot me here. That would be a mess she isn't prepared to clean up inside her fami-ly's vacation home. It would mean finding a store in the middle of nowhere and purchasing things like new paint and bleach. Explaining to her parents why she needs to be the one to clean out the family cabin, not the maid.

She wants to use the threat of that gun to get me to a convenient place so she can shoot me there.

Maybe, if I come out swinging, I can run out the front door and over to the neighbor's. They're a couple miles away.

I might be able to escape.

I stop recording and head into the closet with my phone.

CHAPTER 54

BLAKE
Present Day

The video finishes.

Missy rests her head against the wall, then kicks the corpse next to her. Joy slides just a little.

"I didn't do it, though. I didn't kill Joy," she says over and over as I slip the phone back into my backpack.

"Just like Audrey tried to tell you she didn't kill your husband. But you didn't believe her either. There's a video of that one, too. Do you want to see it? I can bring the phone back out. But instead of believing her, you told Joy to kill the bitch, and you even provided the gun."

"Look." She points to the lump of clothes sitting in the hallway. "Your boyfriend killed Joy. That's his sweat-shirt over there, isn't it?"

Out of the corner of my eye, I see Corbin's sweat-pants and sweatshirt sitting in a lump behind me, covered in blood. It sure is taking him a long time to get those zip ties.

"He lied to you like he lied to me. He was supposed to be here *next* weekend with Ryan and CJ," she says. "Joy barely knew him. Ben was a friend of a friend. Do you even know your own boyfriend?"

She's desperate now, saying whatever will get her out of this.

"All I know," she goes on, her voice rising to a new level, "is I'm pretty sure I was drugged. Joy too. I'm still in my jeans. I don't *sleep* in jeans. My God, it had to be the soup. It was Ben or Corbin. Or whatever the hell he's going by this week…"

"No, it wasn't."

She eyes my knife. "You have to believe me. Don't let him kill me, please. I have kids."

I squat down and lean in. "Your kids are the only reason we're going to let the police decide this, Missy," I say. "Because they deserve a mom. But we all know you helped kill Audrey three years ago and then you killed your friend Joy. So enjoy *parenting* from prison. Maybe you can make a YouTube video out of it. I'm sure your kids will visit you. Enjoy losing your business, your reputation, your house, your career…"

The attic creaks and I look up. It's enough. She reaches behind her back and pulls out a knife I didn't know she had, and lunges at me with it.

I jerk away, stumbling back onto the floorboards, trying to brace myself to get up, but my hand slips in Joy's sticky blood.

I reach for the back wall, using it as leverage to throw

myself forward, shoving the knife into Missy's heart before she gets the chance to stand.

She looks up at me, her eyes glossing over as she falls back, clutching at the knife sticking out of her chest, blood oozing everywhere, then gushing fast.

"You were right about the drugging and the soup," I say. "But you were wrong about which one of us did it."

I motion to Joy. "And you were both wrong when you thought nobody cared about Audrey. I'll let you in on a little secret. I know you didn't kill Joy… because I did, *bitch*. Fuck you for thinking nobody cared."

I pull my necklace out from its tucked-in spot under my sweatshirt so the beetle pendant dangles in her face as I lean over her body. I reach into her pocket and dig out the ring. "I'm going to need this back. You understand, right? It's part of a matching set that belonged to my grandmother."

I take the ring to the sink and turn the water on, waiting for it to warm up. Then, I run my hands into the stream, rinsing the ring off too, watching as the water goes from pink to clear.

My DNA is everywhere, and I really didn't want that.

I never think anything through. Act first. Think second. Story of my life. And no one's around to bail me out this time.

I'll just tell Corbin the truth.

She lunged at me, and I had to kill her… *while I was waiting a year and a half for you to get those zip ties.*

I dry the ring off and slip it into my pocket, just as I hear the backdoor open and the hallway floorboards creak.

I look over. It's Corbin, holding his butcher knife and the box of zip ties. Both hands shake.

"Don't move," he says.

But I don't listen. I walk across the kitchen.

He drops the zip ties and waves the knife at me. "Put your hands where I can see them, Blake. And don't move."

"Corbin, I had to kill her. She lunged at me. It was straight out of a horror movie…"

He's backing up into the hall now. *How did I ever think he could have killed Audrey? He's not even capable of protecting himself.*

I am walking toward him, while he swings the knife in a crazy wild way that looks like he might lose a finger if he's not careful.

"I heard everything, Blake," he yells, inching closer to the backdoor. "You murdered Joy."

My mouth drops.

"Yeah, I heard it."

I turn my head to the side. "How did you hear that, Corbin?"

I didn't yell that to Missy.

He points his knife upward, and I follow its direction to a small decorative shelf sitting above his pair of skis in the corner by the backdoor. I squint at the fake plant there. In between the leaves, there's a clunky white baby monitor… that looks exactly like the video display part in the attic. The extension cord dangles down to the outlet there.

"You were the noise in the attic? I knew someone could climb that tree, pull the scarf off…"

"*And* I recorded everything on my phone from the video monitor," he says. "I thought Missy was going to be the one to confess tonight. I never thought it'd be *you*."

"We need to talk, Corbin."

He drops the knife and runs out the back door into the darkness… because the man really hasn't seen even one horror movie in his life.

And that was the wrong time for a confrontation.

I slowly put on my coat and the bloody ski boots sitting under the coat rack.

Then, I grab the skis and poles by the backdoor, so I can be right behind him.

He doesn't know that Missy and Joy aren't even the first people I've murdered before.

CHAPTER 55

BLAKE
10 Years Old

"Time to grab your shit bucket," Ma'am says as I set the pencil down, closing it into the Bible like a bookmark. Audrey's last message burns in my mind.

GUNINCLOSET

BUTDONTDOIT

WENEEDPLAN

We need a plan. We need a plan.

I wouldn't even be here, stuck in a closet for the rest of my life, if it weren't for her and her plans.

Did she really think Ma'am and Mr. Paul weren't going to figure out how their drugs mysteriously got into the middle school lockers?

She's just lucky one of those kids' parents deals drugs, so it didn't come back to us, or we'd both be dead.

Sometimes, I think I'd be better off that way.

Audrey used to look out for me. But there's nothing she can do now, when Ma'am's passed out and Mr. Paul comes down the hall with a candy bar behind his back.

"Your sister's getting too old for me," he told me last week. He had a smile when he said it, like he thought I'd be happy to hear that. *"You'll be getting all these candy bars soon."*

"What did you learn today?" Ma'am asks, untying my hand from the back of the chair.

"Bad company corrupts good character," I say. I've said this verse to her before. It's one of her favorites, and I can tell it fits here. We both know I am being punished because of Audrey's actions. She's happy I've learned something about it.

"That's right. It's good to lean on the scriptures." She nods and leads me over to the bathroom.

One hour a day to wash ourselves and study the Bible, and the cleaning part's not every day. That's all the time we have out of the closet. And we don't even get to do that together, because Ma'am doesn't trust us when we're together.

I'm going crazy. Audrey knows it. I've told her. It's all I ever write to her.

THINKOFSOMETHING

I'm done waiting. She knew there had to be a gun in that locked closet. She just needed a distraction to find out because they never leave her alone.

"Sorry, I passed out earlier," I say, looking up at Ma'am as I grab my still-wet bucket from the shower.

"That's okay. The noise just scared me, that's all," she replies.

I can tell she likes me. I am the good one. She actually leaves me alone in her room when she needs to use the toilet or grab some more wine while I'm reading the Bible.

She trusts me.

Which is why I'm not waiting for Audrey to think of something. It has to be me. It has to be now.

They won't be expecting it.

Fortunately, my sweatpants and sweatshirt are baggy, and Ma'am doesn't notice anything in my pocket when she leads me back to my closet, even though the gun is heavier than I thought it'd be and it makes my pants slip.

She opens the door, revealing the dark stuffiness that is all I have right now.

I set my bucket down in the corner, but wait to pull out the gun until I hear all three bolts locking on the other side of the closet and footsteps hustling away.

I'm only 80 percent sure this thing is loaded. And I have never used one of these before.

But I will figure it out by the time Mr. Paul comes with his candy bar.

CHAPTER 56

BLAKE
Present Day

I check the cellar and the shed first, then slowly move onto the patch of trees that surrounds the cabin. Corbin is out here somewhere.

And I want him to know I'm with him the entire way. We are a couple. We can get past this.

I squint at the darkness. It's not dawn yet, but it will be soon. Still, I'm surprised by how well I can see with moonlight reflecting off the snow.

I've never skied before. Corbin was right, though. It *is* a lot like skating once you get the hang of it.

It doesn't take long for me to figure out how to go faster by continually shifting my weight a little, gliding from side to side.

The hockey lessons my adopted family had me take when I was 11 are finally paying off.

Every once in a while, I hear my boyfriend panting in the woods beside me, running from tree to tree. He's not quiet. But then, he's more like trudge-running, which can't be easy. Sometimes, I throw a rock in his direction, just to keep him moving with me.

"I only want to talk, Corbin," I call out. "I just wanted to make sure you didn't have anything to do with Audrey's disappearance. You have to admit, you were acting strange all weekend. But I know you didn't have anything to do with it now."

He does not want to talk to me, not sure why. I've never hurt him, and we can clear everything up if we try.

Plus, he has to know I can blame everything on him. I'm sure the smoking-gun video of me confessing is grainy and awful.

It was taken on an iPhone, recording a baby monitor from 1996 in a dimly lit attic. I replay my conversation with Missy in my head. The bulk of his video must be her, trying to talk me into believing he'd done it.

I can see why she thought that, too.

His sweatshirt and sweatpants, that I took from the duffle bag before I kicked him out of the room last night, are clearly the clothes the murderer was wearing when they killed Joy. They're sitting right in the hall, in the spot where Missy pointed them out to me.

I didn't wear them to frame Corbin, but they do support a different version of events now.

I stop ski-skating and toss another rock into the patch of trees to the side of me, making Corbin gasp and run faster. I let him get ahead, then ski to catch up.

Where is he running to? Does he even have a plan?

I'm mainly keeping an eye on him to make sure he's safe.

It's the least I can do. It's dark and we're in the middle of nowhere in a snowstorm. He told me himself that it's not a good idea to be alone out here. You can easily fall into a well, get hypothermia, or wake up a hibernating bear or something if you're not careful.

After a while, I finally see it. He's been running toward a cabin in the distance. There's a light there.

That has to be the neighbor he talked about before. If I make it there first, I can get a jump on my "he did this" story that I'll definitely be using as leverage if Corbin doesn't work with me.

I ski ahead, leaving my boyfriend behind. My adrenalin pumps faster the closer I get to the small wooden house, as I rehearse what I'm going to say in my head.

I unclip my skis, resting them on the banister of the porch and head up to the front door. I waste no time, in case they have a camera. I have to look like I'm frantic.

It feels good to set my backpack down for a second as I pound on the door. One fist after the other. "Please. Please," I yell. "I think he's right behind me. Hurry."

No one answers. So I repeat myself. This time, with even more urgency. I look around.

Just like when I was stuck on the porch outside our cabin, I think about breaking a window. But that might not come across the way I want it to. Homeowners don't like that in a snowstorm.

I try the knob first, surprised when it opens. I scoop my backpack up and step inside.

The place is dark. I hit the light switch by the door,

but nothing happens. "Hello, hello," I say, calling into the cabin, my voice echoing off the walls.

I look around for a phone.

A dark shadow emerges from the hallway, and I take a step back toward the still-opened door, remembering now how Corbin said the neighbor was strange.

The man flicks on a light, but only one lamp turns on, creating a dim orange cast that only kind of glows into the room, barely lighting the place.

"I'm so sorry to disturb you," I say, forgetting everything else I'd rehearsed earlier. "I... was just hoping to use your phone. Can you please call 911? I'll wait outside. I'm gonna wait outside, actually. I shouldn't be here."

I don't turn to leave. I back up.

There isn't much to this living room, just a couple of couches, a single lamp on one of the end tables, and some old portrait photos from about fifteen years ago where a man... *this* man, probably... sits next to a young boy with freckles.

Lots of freckles and blonde hair. It hits me, and I rethink everything.

Was I the one leading Corbin here, or was he leading me?

Because that boy is Corbin.

And I hear the sound of footsteps coming up the porch behind me.

CHAPTER 57

I turn.

Corbin is there, right there, his face twisted and sweaty. It almost seems to glow in the moonlight. Worse than the time in the cellar. He pulls his hood back and blinks at me, his hair moist and matted to his head.

He looks like a man who belongs in this house.

He's breathing hard from the run through the snow. He grabs the door frame and bends forward, trying to catch his breath.

I'm already reaching behind my back, my fingers fumbling to find the part of my backpack with the knife in it. "I can explain," I say, as I tug on a zipper.

He sees me doing it and shakes his head, charging toward me, lunging at me with both arms out.

I duck away, smacking my hand against one of the picture frames on the end table. Pain shoots over my fingers, but I manage to grab the frame.

The shadowy figure is walking into the room now, too. And I don't like how slowly he's coming.

He has a plan.

Two against one.

I swing the frame in Corbin's direction. "This is you. This is… you."

He doesn't answer.

I step forward as I swing. The frame makes a whooshing sound in front of me as I try to create a path to the door.

But he senses this and moves to block it, slamming the door shut.

I have nowhere to go but the back wall. I inch my way over, realizing I'm cornered, except for the window to my side. If I get a running start, I can break through to the porch.

"We should talk," I say, still swinging the frame around.

"There's nothing to talk about."

"Cory, what's going on?" the man says.

Cory?

And that's when I hear it. The sound of a gun cocking. I turn. The guy steps into the light, and I see it now. He has a gun, aimed right at my head.

And I know firsthand what guns can do.

But I also know how to play the part of the "good girl" until everyone lets their guard down enough for me to make an escape.

"Okay, okay," I say, holding my hands up. "For the record, I wasn't trying to hurt you."

"Set the frame down, hand me your backpack, and

put your hands behind your back," Corbin instructs in a voice I don't recognize. He reaches in his pocket, tossing a handful of zip ties on the couch beside me.

My shoulders relax a little when I see those little plastic restraints curled along the dark cushion.

"Tell me what's going on, Corbin. Or Cory. Or is it Ben? Why were you snooping in the attic? Why were you even at the cabin in the first place?" I ask.

I look at the portrait again as I set it on the couch next to the zip ties. He is about eleven or twelve. Just him and his dad. The guy over there with the gun.

I hand him my backpack. He practically snatches it from my fingers, but he doesn't answer my questions.

So I continue trying to piece it together myself. "We both know *that man* over there — the neighbor you told me was crazy — is really your *father*," I add. "You grew up a couple miles from Joy's? The little boy in that picture is you." I don't say I can tell by all the freckles, but I can. It's pretty apparent.

Freckles. *Freckles*. I look him in the eye now. I'm pretty sure I know who he is.

Corbin yanks my hands behind me. I twist my palms so they angle out slightly when he zips the ties shut.

"It's going to look like you did it, *Freckles*. You know that, right? You don't think the police are going to figure out that you're the kid in that old Missy Lagdon video? The Makeup for Freckles one."

He pulls the zip tie so tight my wrists hurt. The plastic digs into my skin. I shift my hand a little to give it more room.

"*I* figured it out in half a minute, *Cory*. *They* will, too, unless we give the police a reason not to look too hard. We can help each other."

Once I'm tied, he sits on the couch next to me and rests his face in his hands.

"I remember it," I say. "They tortured you in that video. It wasn't funny. They ruined your life for a few million likes. It was all over my elementary school. Your face was one of the first memes. I can see why you moved to the middle of nowhere, so no one would know you."

His dad puts the gun down. "Looks like you have this, Cory. Let me know if you need me," he says and disappears into the hallway again.

"Missy wasn't a nice person," I add.

He rubs his eyes with the lower part of his palms. "Neither was Joy. They were both there."

It all made sense. The rats, the roaches, the ghosts. This man wasn't a killer. He was still that little boy, looking for revenge on his bullies.

I was the only killer here.

"Did you move near Joy to get her back? Sneak into the attic? Was that… was that you?"

"Yeah. I ruined her family's whole rental business when I was a kid. Putting crumbs all over the place, then finding rats to put in there with them. Wasn't long before they were known for running a roach motel."

"Nice."

A ghost of a smile escapes his lips.

"I even took a job down the street from Lagdon Marketing when I got older," he says, "and befriended a couple of guys there. Ryan and CJ. I guess I wanted to see if I could ruin Joy and Missy's lives as adults. They never recognized me or remembered me. I even went on a few skiing trips with them. Stayed in Joy's cabin. They never made the connection. Of course, I told them my name was Ben. And when they were making that video, they knew me as Freckles. Or Cory."

He looks up at the ceiling as he talks. I can't tell if it feels good for him to get this off his chest or not. I can tell I'm probably the first person he's ever told this to. The only one who knows, besides his dad.

And it occurs to me that's not a good thing here. Once again, I think about hiding my phone some place.

"But the worst thing I could get myself to do was key their cars once," he says with an exasperated chuckle. "And I'm not even sure I got Missy's. I was still doing kid things. I couldn't get myself out of kid mode when I was around them."

I scoot closer to him. I want to hug him, but I can't.

He scoots away, anyway. "One time, Ryan and CJ had a girl with them when they came up to the cabin. That was the time Missy made us all leave early, and then I heard that girl disappeared. They said she was a murderer. They said she ran away. They weren't even going to tell the police she was up here. I was the one who called and left an anonymous tip that she was seen skiing between the old mill and the resort. I never saw her skiing. But I wanted them to have the exact location for Joy's cabin. They never checked it."

He shrugs. "I forgot all about it until I found out from the guys that Joy's family was selling the cabin. I knew it was my last shot to just poke around and see if I found anything incriminating." He shakes his head. "Oh how I wanted to find something that would put them away forever."

"That's why you didn't want me to go with you."

"It's why I came up a week early, too. We were all supposed to come up next week. But I couldn't snoop around with everyone else there. I wasn't even sure I could still get in through the attic. But I did. I was looking for something to tie them to Audrey's disappearance. I was also going to set up the old baby monitor I used to use when I was spying as a kid just to see if I could catch them confessing to something…"

"And you found the room in the cellar," I say.

"Yeah, I knew as soon as I saw that room that it had to be the place. I wasn't sure if they were able to get rid of all the evidence over the years, but I was hoping to find something. They were never going to know who had knocked down that wall because I wasn't supposed to be here until next week. But that glass in the sink made me worry that someone else was here. So I skied down the hill to make sure, and that's when I saw their car. They were coming up a week early, too."

"No wonder they were so mad to see us."

"You only know the half of it, too. After you went upstairs, they berated me for a long time. It felt like I was ten years old all over again. Then they went into the cellar themselves and saw the hole. They came back ready to kill me, I think. Until we all had soup and fell asleep."

He shoots me a knowing look. His hair falls over his hazel eyes in a weird, sweaty lump. All I want to do is brush it away and press my lips over his. But I can't.

"I heard you say you drugged the soup," he says, his

eyes darting up to the ceiling again. "Just tell me why you did it. I guess it's not going to matter because you're right." He runs a hand through his hair, then down his face. "The police are going to think I murdered everyone once they find out who I am."

I shake my head. "Not if we work together. I've actually been down this road before. Audrey Randall was my sister."

"What?" He turns so he's fully facing me. "You don't have a sister. You have three brothers. I've met them. They hate me."

"Adopted brothers. And they don't hate you, Corbin."

He smiles. I can tell he's happy to have something on me now, too. Something he can tell the police. Someone to blame. And I *am* the one in zip ties.

Maybe I should have waited to confess all of this. I was never good at making plans.

"I have another confession, too…" I lean back against the couch cushion and try to get comfortable in my zip ties.

I take a deep breath. This is the first time I've ever admitted any of this to anyone. I didn't tell my adopted family. Or the therapist they had me go to. Nobody.

"I've killed before," I blurt out. "But only because I had to. I had to."

CHAPTER 58

BLAKE
AGE 10

I hear him coming. I've memorized how his footsteps sound on the floorboards in the hall. They're heavier than Ma'am's. Plus, she's always in a hurry. And Mister Paul takes his time.

He tries to be sneaky, stopping every once in a while. Sometimes I wonder if maybe he feels guilty and is trying to talk himself out of it.

He never does.

Ma'am won't wake up tonight. She's had two bottles of wine, at least. I could hear them getting drunk and sloppy, saying they should break open another bottle, laughing while they watch their shows.

There's supposed to be a lady who comes and inspects the living conditions for us. But Audrey and I haven't seen her since she dropped us off here at the trailer in the middle of nowhere.

Nobody comes, except their adult son sometimes. Nobody cares about any of us.

The gun sits heavy in my sweaty palm, and I worry that it's going to slip out, drop to the floor, and go off early if I'm not careful.

I think I've got all the movements memorized, but what if I do it wrong?

I hear the first latch go. Then the second. My heart beats fast in my sweatshirt, so fast it feels like it's going to escape out of my throat. I try to swallow it down.

The third latch unlocks, and there he is.

I don't know what Mister Paul's age is, but he looks old. His hair is real thin, like it doesn't cover his head right. He's skinny as a rail, too.

"Come on out, honey," he whispers to me. "I've got a candy bar here if you're good."

I take a step out, my hand behind my back. My closet is the one in the room that used to be our bedroom. Ma'am uses it to store her stuff now that Audrey and I live in closets.

"That's a good girl," he says as he sets the Snickers bar on one of the stacked boxes and unzips his pants.

While he's looking down, I take out the gun and raise it to his head.

But I don't give him time to react or yell or plead for his life. I just want him to look up and see it. I've practiced this, so I know I cannot give him time. He's much bigger than me. And he thinks he's much smarter.

He finally raises his head, and I pull the trigger immediately, surprised by how powerful the gun is, and how loud. It's crazy loud. It feels like my ears are bleeding, and maybe they are.

Blood is everywhere, along my sweatshirt, splattered all down my chest and on my sweatpants. The gun flies out of my hand from the force of the bullet just as Ma'am bolts through the door.

She screams. *"What in the fuck? What in the fucccck? Ohmygod, you little bitch."*

She looks around, sees me scrambling to pick up the gun, and shoves me out of the way so she can get it.

But I kick her, square in the knee, so hard I hear her bones crack back as she falls to the floor. Then I pick up the gun and shoot her in the head while she's down.

But there's so much blood. Too much blood. I am covered in it. The room. My sweatshirt. It's all in my hair. I smell it dripping off the walls.

I wasn't expecting this.

And my ears are still ringing, like an awful loud squeal. But just above it, I hear Audrey's voice, screaming, "Blake, are you okay? Blake? Answer me."

"I'm okay," I manage. "I did it, Audrey. I did it. They can't hurt us anymore."

"I know you did. Come unlock my closet."

Audrey's closet is the one in the hall. I have to stand on my toes to get all three latches unlocked.

She assesses the situation, looking at the mess. The blood smeared on her closet latch, in the hall, in the back bedroom. Me, with bloody hands covering my ears because I can't stop the ringing.

She's always been good at looking at things and coming up with a plan.

"Go wash your hands and all the blood off your hair and stuff," she says.

But I can't move. I'm frozen to my spot.

"Now. Go! Wash them seven times, with soap… each time. And use the hottest water you can stand. Then we've gotta change clothes. Those sweats are so baggy on you, I can fit in them. We'll put the gun in Ma'am's hand. We'll tell the police that she shot Mr. Paul when she saw him about to do something with one of her foster kids, then she shot herself. A murder-suicide."

"What if they don't believe us?"

She looks around. "They probably won't. I've seen Forensic Files back when Mom used to watch it. They can tell what happened by looking at the scene. They'll know one of us really did this. But if it's gotta be one of us, it's gotta be me. I'll be the one to go off to juvie. That's why you need to go wash your hands. Right now. It's also why we gotta switch clothes. You can't have gun residue on your hands or clothes. They check."

As soon as we've switched clothes, Audrey shoots the gun again, only she aims for the floor. "I'll have the gun residue on me now."

Tears roll down my cheeks. "I don't want you to get in trouble."

"No, Blake. I was the one who got us into this mess. I was the reason we had to go to foster care in the first place. Mom wouldn't have almost killed her boyfriend with that baseball bat if I hadn't taken Grandma's jewelry. And I was the reason we got locked in the closets, too. You are the one who got us out. You *are* the good one. You'll always be the good one. You'll get adopted, you'll see. You're still plenty young enough, now that the state won't try to keep us together. It'll all work out. Just… go wash your hands. I got this. They can't hurt us anymore."

CHAPTER 59

BLAKE
Present Day

Corbin has moved closer to me on the couch. He kisses my forehead, and for a brief moment, it feels like things are back to normal.

Because I do love this man.

I wasn't sure before. I needed to know if he was involved with my sister's disappearance before I could truly love him.

It was why I bumped into him at the coffee shop last year. It took me a while to find the "local kid" the people at the Olsen Mart told me they saw with Audrey after I posted all those missing-person posters around here.

But then, I really did fall in love with him. There was just something about him. He was weird, like me. And that counts in so many more ways than anything else in life.

"Looks like we're both going to jail," he says.

"No, Corbin. I told you that story, not just so you'll know why I did what I did back at the cabin. But so you'll also know there's a way out of this if we get the puzzle to look right. The police only check your story if the crime scene looks different from your story."

I tell him about Audrey's phone in my backpack, about the video I showed to Missy (apparently before he got up to the attic), and about how we can change the iPhone's passcode to something simple like 1234 so the police will know how Missy got in.

"Then we'll put it on the floor by Missy's feet and show them why she killed Joy. She found out Joy was the one who killed her husband, not Audrey. And I had to kill Missy when she attacked me, after I reminded her that she just lost everything, because that part is true."

Audrey would be proud that I'm coming up with a plan. She was always the one who insisted on those. And it's the least I can do for her now.

"I promise you, Corbin. If we do this right, they'll never check who we are."

Corbin has me tell him the story again and again, then points to my arms still tied behind my back. "I'm so sorry. Let me get you out of those zip ties. They must hurt."

I lift my hands to show him I was already out.

BLAKE
Seven Months Later...

Corbin reaches across the console and puts his hand on my shoulder as we pull up to the iron gates of the cemetery. It's a nice spot. Exactly what my sister deserves.

We follow the twisting road leading around the mausoleum and over to the tree where Audrey's grave marker is located. It didn't take long for the police to find some of her remains in the locked part of the cellar that weekend.

Joy had apparently tried to dispose of everything beforehand and was just coming up to make sure she got it all. She hadn't. She missed quite a few items of Audrey's that I'm sure my sister hid in various parts of the room before she passed.

I hate it that Audrey died being trapped in a closet all over again. Just when we'd both broken free from that.

To make matters worse, I couldn't claim any of the remains without raising eyebrows. But the whole town got together and bought her this gravestone.

And I made sure she was buried with her beetle ring, sneaking it in at the end of the ceremony the town held for her.

Corbin parks and we both get out. The sun warms my shoulders. A far cry from the snowed-in weekend I spent at the cabin seven months ago. It's the kind of day my sister would have loved.

Her Bible codes were always trying to calm me down when we were little.

WEWILLGETOUT

STOPWORRYING

PICTUREAGOODDAY

My engagement ring-wedding band combo sparkles in the sunlight. It's perfect, just like my husband.

After Corbin proposed, we got married right away in a small ceremony up in Bear Landing with pretty much just my parents and brothers. And his dad.

It was all we could afford, but it was also all we needed.

He pulls me in closer and I smile into his button-down shirt. The bouquet of wildflowers I bought for Audrey scratches at my arm a little.

"Do you want to do this alone?" he asks.

I nod. He always knows what I need in life. Ten-year-old me, locked in her closet, would never have imagined being married to someone like Corbin.

He even brought the soup up that weekend. He hadn't found it in the cellar. It was why his backpack was so heavy. He was making sure we had food because he had no idea what the cabin was like anymore. Always the Boy Scout.

I walk over to Audrey's grave, leaving my husband back by the car, and place the bouquet into the little spot for flowers.

"I have a lot to tell you," I say to the headstone, like she can hear me in there.

"I'm married now." I pat my belly. "And pregnant. Twelve weeks along. I worry a lot that I won't be a good mom. We didn't have too many examples of those in our life." I laugh like that's funny, mostly because if I don't laugh, I'll cry.

My sundress blows in the late summer breeze. It's a little colder up here than it is in the desert. Just another thing I'll have to get used to.

"Thank you for doing all you did for me so long ago. Not just the obvious stuff. Finding the gun. Taking the blame. Calming me down every time I got antsy. Getting me the beetle necklace when Mom would have traded it for meth. But everything else, too. I know you were only three years older, but you were the mom I'm so thankful I had."

There are strangers not too far from me, paying their respects to their own grave down the way a little. I know they can't hear me, but I still squat down so I'm right by Audrey's headstone and whisper, "You were right. I did get adopted. By the Wallaces. I have three brothers now, who love hockey and hate horror movies. I wish you could meet them.

"But just know that I never forgot you. I looked for you when I got old enough. But you never did social media. You didn't leave me any clues. Then, high school finished, and I went off to college and I thought I had all the time in the world to find you. I didn't find you until you made the news, and by then, it was too late."

A few pine needles and leaves have fallen onto her grave. I mindlessly brush them off, so it looks as perfect as I can get it again. "I found your clues. I always knew you had nothing to do with that murder. Don't worry, I took care of Joy and Missy."

I don't tell her how I drugged everyone's soup using the meds in my backpack. It almost hadn't worked. Thank God Corbin hadn't been the only one to eat that.

Come to find out, he hadn't drugged my soup that night, but my paranoia about it had given me the idea to do it myself so I could watch the videos and figure things out.

I also don't mention that I pretty much killed Joy in cold blood. I didn't tell Corbin that one, either. It's better if he thinks it happened during a struggle when I confronted Joy about Audrey.

I *did* confront her. That part is true. She just didn't even seem regretful when she told me all the things she'd done to Audrey.

How she rented a car and followed her around so she'd know where Audrey lived, because she wasn't sure if she was going to kill Jordan or Audrey. Harassing her. Tormenting her.

Joy's voice was almost giddy when she told me how

happy she was to kill them both. Shooting Audrey in the leg when she ran away at the cabin, then putting her in that room, to rot on her own.

Funny how much people will confess to you when you've got a knife to their throat and they think you're just going to call the cops on them.

She didn't know, until right before the end, that somebody did care about Audrey, and that person was me.

"I learned from the best," I say to my sister.

I open my purse and fumble around to find the paper I put in there.

"There's so much more I want to tell you," I say as I pull out a thin page torn straight from the Bible.

I shove it into the spot by the flowers and kiss her grave, then use the headstone as leverage to pull myself up to a standing position again. "But you can read it yourself. Thanks for making it all possible." I walk back to Corbin.

"You're already done?" he asks when I reach the car.

I nod. "I have to use the bathroom again." It's not a lie. I always have to use the bathroom now.

I get in the jeep, and we head back up the hill. He doesn't point to the Olsen Mart when we pass it, even though we both know I could use that bathroom in an emergency.

We avoid those people.

They clearly recognized me as the woman who stapled the missing-person poster to their bulletin board years ago.

They were the ones who told me they saw Audrey

with three men, but only recognized one. A local boy named Corbin who'd moved to Middleton.

It was why I didn't want to stop at that mini-mart seven months ago, but it was our only option in the snow.

And Corbin hadn't wanted to go in either, because he knew the Olsens would recognize him, too.

Turns out, Corbin and I were both hiding who we were in life. He didn't want me to meet his dad because everything about the viral Makeup for Freckles video might come out. And he'd spent most of his life hiding that from the world.

It's why the ring was in his backpack for so long.

We keep driving up the hill, past that 1996 cabin, and over to the one we bought just down the way from Corbin's dad that looks exactly like Joy's, minus the root cellar.

All the houses are going for a steal around here, now that the ski resort is closed, and the murders made the news.

After Corbin and I cleaned and staged everything that night, we both dealt with the police. We had to, in case they checked fingerprints and DNA at the cabin.

But they never did. And they never once asked who we were.

Because our story checked out.

"Watch your step," Corbin says as he helps me up the porch to our cabin. I am only three months pregnant, but he treats me like I'm made of glass.

I love that about him. He's going to be a great dad.

And my parents are thrilled to be grandparents.

They're not exactly thrilled I'll be hours away from LA. They don't understand why I want to live up in the mountains, but they're okay with making the drive to visit.

They're actually talking about buying a vacation place nearby. I doubt they'll buy Joy's.

I look around at all the 90s decor I chose on purpose. Wood paneling, oversized heavy furniture, fake plants. Even a couple of whittled bears.

Corbin hands me a glass of lemonade as I sit at the dining table. His dad is already on his way over. They're going to start a tech business together, up here in the boonies where tech businesses are probably needed the most.

My parents are pitching in some seed money.

We're not rich, but a part of me knows everything will be okay, as long as we have each other.

I have Audrey to thank for that, for a lot of things in my life, but mostly for showing me what a great family looks like.

And now, like I let my sister know in the Bible pages I placed on her grave, I'm going to make sure my daughter, Audrey, knows what a great family looks like, too.

❧❦❧

HI. E.L. FAIRE HERE. THANK YOU FOR READING MY book. I hope you liked it. If you did, please consider leaving a review and telling your friends. I'd really appreciate it.

If you'd like to know when new releases are coming out, just go to my website, Ettafaire.com, and sign up for my newsletter list. While you're there, you'll also see I write mysteries under Etta Faire.